Buxton Peak
Book Three:
The End of the
Beginning

Julie L. Spencer

ISBN-10:1544852444
ISBN-13:978-1544852447

DEDICATION

Buxton Peak Book Three: The End of the Beginning
is dedicated to all who realize that at the end of every story is
the beginning of another...

CONTENTS

ACKNOWLEDGMENTS

Book Three is a little different than the others in the *Buxton Peak* trilogy. For one, I wrote it twice.

When I got to the end of the story, I realized it was written from the wrong Point of View, so I completely re-wrote it. Not just edited what I'd already written, but started from scratch.

Once I started rewriting, the words just flowed. Having done that, I wish I could go back to square one and rewrite all the rest of the books. Maybe someday.

For now, I love that my readers get to know Ian Taylor through Megan's eyes in *Books One* and *Two*.
We are able to step back and see him as others see him, not just as he sees himself.

You, as the reader, already know that the same acknowledgments apply as all my other books: thank you to my family, friends, beta readers, editors, cover designer, and most importantly, our Heavenly Father.

For now, I hope you enjoy getting to know Ian Taylor even better…

Let's rock! -Julie L. Spencer

CHAPTER ONE:
CONVERSATION WITH A SIDE OF DRUMSTICKS

"Does this guy even know we're coming to his concert tonight?" Ian asked. The waitress had yet to take their orders, but Ian wanted to get down to the real reason they were meeting. He hadn't been together with his band members in months, but they weren't there to have a nice meal with their best girls; this was business.

Andy shrugged and raised his eyebrows. "I've never actually met him."

"What?" Ian leaned forward and pushed his hands against the table, gripping the tablecloth. "How do you know he's a good drummer if you've never heard him play?"

"He plays at their church worship services on Sundays. He's like, a minister, or something."

Andy brushed his shaggy bangs off his forehead, and Ian couldn't help but notice how clear Andy's eyes were and how clean he looked.

Obviously the stylist had recently gotten her hands on Andy's hair. Ian was reminded how long it had been since anyone had worked over him. All the guys tended to let the stylists have free reign with purposefully random highlights and just the right amount of length to keep them looking like the rock stars they were.

Andy had only lived in Nashville for a few weeks, and it surprised Ian that Andy was attending a church at all. His new girlfriend seemed to be a good influence.

Nashville was a good situation all around. Andy needed to get away from the negative influences back in England where he originally became involved with drugs.

When Ian found out Andy met a new drummer, Ian chartered a jet faster than he could pack. They would worry about bringing their furniture down from Michigan later. Ian loved Nashville the minute he arrived.

"So, this drummer just plays in a little *church* band?" Kai shook his head and mumbled under his breath. "What are we doing here?"

"Tonight there's a *real* concert at their church," Andy said. "There will be hundreds of people in attendance."

"We're used to playing for *thousands*," Kai reminded Andy, leaning forward and creasing his eyebrows. "This guy's not even in our league."

"You willing to go back to London and reconcile with Gary?" Andy narrowed his eyes at Kai. "Because the last time I saw him, he was heading back into rehab. I doubt he'll be practicing his drums while he's there. Not to mention, there's the little issue with him having given drugs to your girlfriend. Have you forgiven him yet?"

Kai glanced over, met Rhonda's eyes, and looked down at their baby. A few months ago baby Sean had been delivered seven weeks early. He almost died because of the drugs Gary gave to Rhonda. No, it wouldn't be easy for Kai to forgive Gary no matter how badly the band needed a drummer. Ian pulled the conversation back to the task at hand.

"Okay, so Buxton Peak is shy one drummer, and we all agree we're not bringing Gary back on board?" Ian raised his eyebrows and looked pointedly at Kai and then Andy.

Ian already knew the answer, but it was just a formality anyway. Ian Taylor *owned* Buxton Peak. The band, the name, all of their songs. If he wanted a new drummer, he would hire a new drummer. If he wanted to replace Andy as their bass guitar player, he could. He would never consider replacing Kai as their lead guitar, but the other guys were expendable, and they knew it.

"We gave Gary an ultimatum; get cleaned up or leave the band," Ian said. "Gary made his choice. We're making ours. Let's just show up at Nathanial's concert tonight and see if he's a good fit."

"So, what? We just walk up and steal their drummer?" Kai sounded concerned, but there was a gleam in his eyes. Ian half expected him to reach over and offer a fist bump. Kai knew Ian better than anyone else in the world, probably even better than his wife, Megan, although Ian would never admit that. He wrapped his arm around the back of Megan's chair and grinned at Kai.

Kai Burton was Ian's best friend since primary school. He was also one of the most talented guitar players Ian had ever met. Kai and Ian worked together to build Buxton Peak into the mega-stars they were. They'd been through a lot together and had a non-verbal communication that surpassed most usual relationships. Together, they would find a way to pull their band back together.

"Nathanial's a youth pastor," Vanessa drawled, her southern accent a stark contrast to the guys' British dialects. Ian understood why Andy was drawn to her. She was adorable. Ditzy, but adorable. "I've known him and his wife for years. They have the sweetest little girl."

With longing in her eyes, Vanessa looked down at baby Sean resting in Rhonda's arms. Ian was waiting for Vanessa to beg Andy for a baby the same way a child would beg for a puppy. Andy already seemed serious about Vanessa although they'd only known each other a few months. But he didn't seem to notice her distracted gaze. Andy was focused on music.

The waitress interrupted with baskets of dinner rolls and their drinks. While the others took turns ordering food, Ian spread whipped butter on a warm roll and contemplated this turn of events.

Ian had grown up as the lead singer and songwriter for Buxton Peak. He'd bonded with his band mates like brothers, but they'd never shared the same values. Andy and Gary had spiraled out of control with drinking and drug abuse. Now Andy was a recovering addict, and Gary was leaving the band.

Andy's eyes were clear and confident. He seemed... different. Sobriety suited him. Ian and Andy Smith had connected in their seventh year of school. He was talented on the bass guitar and a great pal. But when he and Gary had gotten involved in drugs and alcohol, it nearly destroyed their band.

Gary hadn't stayed sober. It was too bad, because he was a great drummer. But a rock band as successful as Buxton Peak would bounce back without Gary Owens. This guy, Nathanial might be just what they needed.

"So…" Ian forced the conversation back around after the waitress left. "We're just going to show up tonight at his concert unexpectedly and go up to him afterwards, introduce ourselves, and say, 'Hey, want to get together and jam sometime, mate?' Is that the idea?"

"Pretty much." Andy shoved a bite of roll into his mouth and nodded.

"That's not a bad way to interview someone," Kai pointed out. "If he doesn't know that we're there, then he'll just be acting normal and not trying to show off. You know what I mean?" They all nodded in unison. This could get interesting.

* * * * * * * * *

"We sort of stand out…" Megan whispered, pulling Ian's arm as they climbed out of the car. Ian tucked her hand into the crook of his elbow as if he was escorting a queen to a royal ball rather than walking together into an inner-city, non-denominational church in the heart of Nashville. It wasn't huge, but bigger than most churches Ian and Megan attended. "I've gotten rather used to rural Michigan."

"It is different seeing people do a double-take when they recognize us," Ian acknowledged. "No one paid much attention to us in Mt. Pleasant anymore."

"That's because we haven't been *together* in almost a year," Kai said. He hoisted Sean's baby carrier over his arm and handed the diaper bag to Rhonda. "I'm afraid we're going to start needing bodyguards again."

Ian sighed. They still *weren't* together. They were missing Gary. He wondered if they ever would be together again.

"Bodyguards? We're not a scary church..." Vanessa pouted. "I mean, look at the beautiful diversity of people stepping through those doors. Young, old, all colors and nationalities, rich and poor, and even a couple of rock stars." Vanessa poked Andy in the side and winked at him. He pulled her close and planted a kiss on her forehead. It was nice to see Andy so happy. He deserved some happiness.

"All churches are scary to me." Kai wrinkled his nose. "I don't believe in God."

"Fear and faith cannot exist in the heart at the same time," Vanessa drawled. "You just need to gain some faith, and you won't be afraid anymore."

"Not happening anytime soon," Kai said, rolling his eyes. He held the door for Rhonda, and everyone else tucked in behind her. Ian brought up the rear of the group and patted Kai on the shoulder.

"Someday," Ian whispered.

"Don't count on it, preacher boy."

"Let's sit in the very back and hopefully no one will notice us," Ian said. *Yeah… too late.* "Well, hopefully no one will tell Nathanial we're here, anyway." The band was warmed up and ready to begin. People on the stage came and went, adjusting cords and wires, conversing with one another. The whole scene was casual, laid-back, and relaxed. It was worlds away from a stadium concert with 50,000 screaming fans.

"That's him at the drums," Andy whispered, nodding in the direction of the stage. A tall, black man with a friendly smile and stocky shoulders sat behind an elaborate drum set.

"He's a right big bloke," Ian said. "He looks like he could handle himself in a rugby scrum." Teenagers surrounded Nathanial, and he seemed to enjoy their attention. He smiled and laughed and gave them random fist bumps. *Youth pastor, that's right. Vanessa had mentioned it.* Ian was drawn to him immediately, but followed his little group to the back of the auditorium-style worship center and took a seat.

Once the first song began, Ian couldn't sit still. Before he realized what was happening, he was standing against the back wall with his head close together with Kai and Andy.

"He's good," Kai whispered.

"Really good..." Ian nodded in time with the beat.

"Their bass player is better than I am," Andy acknowledged. Both Ian and Kai looked over at Andy with raised eyebrows.

"We're not looking to replace our bass guitarist," Ian said. "You planning on quitting anytime soon? I could go get the guy's number if you want..."

"I don't think I like the lead singer." Andy changed the subject. "He looks cocky and presumptuous. His facial expressions are over-the-top, like he's trying too hard to look like he's religious, but isn't as much as he pretends to be."

Again, Ian and Kai raised their eyebrows at Andy. "That's deep analysis, pal."

"I've just seen the difference..." Andy shrugged and dismissed their scrutiny. "*You* don't try to be religious, Ian. God's light just shines through all you do. It always has."

Ian couldn't form a coherent response to that. He just stared at Andy with his jaw slacked.

"When did *you* start believing in God," Kai asked.

"I dunno…" Andy shrugged. He scratched his head and looked away. "I'm not sure I do."

"We'll talk another time," Ian told him, clapping him on the back. "For now, let's listen to our new drummer and his soon-to-be-former band mates."

They turned their attention back to Nathanial. Now that Andy had pointed it out, Ian could see what he meant about the lead singer. They were playing cover songs of inspirational Christian rock music. Ian recognized most of the songs, but the front man seemed to be trying too hard. With only three guys on the stage, the lead singer was also their lead guitarist.

Their bass guitarist wore a cowboy hat and boots and looked more as if he belonged in a country band than a Christian band. He seemed very young compared to the lead singer and Nathanial. Andy was right, the bass guitarist was better than he was. But a lot of bassists were better than Andy. He wasn't the reason Buxton Peak was such a successful rock band, but they definitely weren't replacing him.

Ian tried to evaluate Nathanial from afar. He was probably in his mid-to-late twenties, and wore a wedding ring. He was confident and talented, but obviously holding back. Ian wanted to hear him wail on those drums. Nathanial was *not* meant to play in the back of this little

Christian band. Ian pictured him in a stadium full of screaming fans, full out jamming on those drums. He felt drawn to this man in many ways. He sensed they were going to be great friends and kindred spirits.

At intermission, people stood, stretched, conversed, and meandered to the tables with cookies and punch. Ian didn't budge and didn't take his eyes off Nathanial. Kids and adults came and went. A little girl with cornrow braids ran onto the stage and climbed up on Nathanial's lap. Ian assumed she was his daughter. A beautiful woman came up, kissed him, and picked the girl up from her daddy's arms. They talked for a moment, and then the girls walked away.

The moment Ian had assumed would happen finally did. Someone whispered in Nathanial's ear and his head jerked around. Ian raised an eyebrow, and Nathanial's eyes widened. He whispered back to the guy beside him. Ian could tell they were trying to hide their conversation from the other two guys in the band. Nathanial knew exactly why the three remaining members of Buxton Peak were standing in the back of his sanctuary.

Nathanial took a drink from his water bottle and sat at his drum set fiddling with his sticks. Ian half expected him to snap his fingers at the other band members to encourage them to get back into position and resume the show.

Nathanial's knee started bouncing, and he tatted his sticks lightly against the edge of his snare. It wasn't loud enough to get very many people's attention, but he wasn't playing for everyone; he was talking directly to the three guys standing in the back of the room with their arms crossed and light grins on their faces. Nathanial tapped a little louder with a bit more rhythm.

It was obvious Nathanial was showing off. Ian nodded just slightly in time with the drumsticks, and the conversation continued.

Finally, the other band members strapped on their instruments and began the process of tuning the knobs and testing the strings. The audience members returned to their seats after throwing away paper cups of punch and napkins covered in cookie crumbs.

The second half of the show did not disappoint. Nathanial showed no sign of nervousness once the music started. He was in his element, in the same zone Ian performed in. He didn't seem to be over-performing, just playing exactly what he rehearsed hundreds of times with his band. But he had more talent than the other two combined. They were holding him back in more ways than one. He was never going to make it out of Nashville playing with these guys, in this small church, and he was never going to be able to play with his whole soul as long as he was sitting behind them.

The concert ended with a moving ballad that showcased the lead singer's vocal abilities and all of their love and devotion to God. But it didn't satisfy Ian's desire to see Nathanial perform. The anticipation of hearing him play again was almost palpable. Ian couldn't wait to get him in a studio.

CHAPTER TWO: SCANDALOUS

"Nathanial, my man, great job tonight." It took Nathanial a few seconds to realize his lead singer was trying to get his attention, because his eyes were drawn to the back of the room. Steve reached over the drum set to shake his hand. "Nathanial?"

"Oh, sorry." Nathanial leaned forward, shook Steve's hand, and glanced up to the back of the sanctuary again. "Yeah, great show…"

"You okay?" Steve creased his eyebrows. He glanced over his shoulder for a second, but turned back, a concerned frown on his face. "Whatcha lookin' at, buddy?"

"Nothin'…" Nathanial was pretty sure Steve hadn't turned long enough to focus all the way to the back of the room. His heart started pounding. *How long should I postpone the inevitable? I should tell him now.*

No! I don't even know why they're here. I'm not going to jump to any conclusions. They could just be here to see a good concert. They could be here because they're passing through Nashville on the way to their next tour dates.

Oh, who am I kidding? There could only be one reason why they would come here… without Gary. They're here for me. I know it. I just know it.

What am I supposed to do now? Wait for them to come talk to me? Go introduce myself?

While he had his internal conversation, Nathanial gathered his things. The towel he dropped on the floor after wiping his brow—he shoved it in his duffle bag. The two empty water bottles—he set those to the back of the stage where someone would take them to the kitchen and put them in the recycling bin. He tucked his drumsticks in the inside pocket of his suit coat. He didn't have to wait long. *Here they come.*

Nathanial mirrored Ian's smirk as he held eye contact the whole way down the aisle. They ascended the stairs and the four men faced each other in a small square. Ian reached out and ran his fingers along the edge of the hanging symbol.

"Quite a nice setup you got here, mate," Ian whispered. He never broke eye contact.

"Thanks, brotha'." Nathanial had been a fan of Buxton Peak for years. He even saw them in concert once. He knew their music, he knew the rumors about their drummer in rehab, he knew there was the possibility they'd be looking for someone new. He never dreamed it would be *him*.

"Oh… my… gosh!" The silence was broken when Ryan turned around with his bass guitar still strapped around his shoulder. Ryan's enthusiastic recognition clued in Steve that there were three extra people on the stage, and he turned as well.

"Hello there." Steve tilted his head to the side and creased his brow. "I'm not sure we've met. Are you new to the area?"

"Steve…" Nathanial cleared his throat. "This is Ian Taylor, Kai Burton, and Andy Smith… from Buxton Peak."

"Pleasure to meet you." Steve stepped closer to shake their hands.

"Likewise," Ian said, reaching out his hand.

"Very nice show, mate." Kai nodded.

"We enjoyed it very much," Andy said. After he shook Steve's hand, Andy reached over to Ryan as well. "You're a very good bassist. Nice job."

"Oh my gosh! Thank you *so* much!" Ryan pumped Andy's arm with childlike enthusiasm.

"You must be from England," Steve said. "You all have British accents. What brings you to Nashville?"

"Nathanial." Ian didn't crack a smile, and he didn't break eye contact with Steve.

"Oh, that's great you were able to see your friend in concert." Steve nodded and reached over to clap Nathanial on the shoulder. Ian raised his eyebrows. "How long have you known Nathanial?"

"About two minutes," Ian said and then cocked his head to the side. "In fact, I don't think we've ever actually been formally introduced... I'm Ian Taylor." Ian, whose now-familiar smirk pulled at the corner of his mouth, reached out and shook hands with Nathanial.

"Nathanial Jackson," he responded, mirroring Ian's expression. "Welcome to Nashville."

"It's a pleasure to be here." They nodded in unison.

"Wait, if you've never actually met..." Steve hesitated. "What *are* you doing here?"

"These guys are from Buxton Peak, Steve." Ryan's smile fell, and he gulped. Ryan had figured it out.

"Oh, is Buxton Peak in England?" Steve cocked his head to the side. *He doesn't know who they are.* Nathanial forgot Steve wasn't a fan of mainstream music.

"Steve," Nathanial interrupted. "Buxton Peak is a band. A very famous rock band. I mean, yeah, it's technically named after the *town* of

Buxton… right? Surrounded by the High Peak forest, right?" Nathanial found himself rambling.

"Close enough." Ian waved his hand dismissively.

"Are you in America doing a concert tour?" Steve smiled again.

"Let's dispense with the formalities, mate… We're here to steal your drummer." Ian stated it simply, as if it should have been obvious by now.

"Wh… what?" Steve's face grew red. He pursed his lips together and held his chin high. "Nathanial already has a band… with us."

"Steve…" Nathanial shook his head, reached over, and put his hand on Steve's arm. "I'm sorry. I can't pass this up." Steve yanked his arm away and glared over at Ian, who tucked his hands in his pockets and shrugged.

"Hey, can I get your autographs?" Ryan broke the tension again. He lifted the strap off his shoulder and handed his bass guitar directly to Andy, along with a Sharpie marker. Andy signed the guitar in big, scrawling letters and handed the bass to Kai. After Kai signed it, he handed the guitar and marker to Ian, who leaned over and wrote his name with firm confidence. He handed the bass guitar back to Ryan and turned to Steve, who had his electric guitar resting in its stand next to him.

"Would you like yours signed as well, mate?"

Ian asked, twirling the Sharpie in his right hand as he would a drumstick. He raised his eyebrows. Nathanial would have laughed at the situation if Steve wasn't shaking and turning red. He stormed off the stage, almost knocking over Nathanial's daughter, Taisha and her friend, Jenny.

Taisha jumped into her daddy's arms and wrapped her little hands around his big shoulders. "Can I stay the night at Jenny's house?"

"Taisha, I'd like you to meet a few of my friends," Nathanial told her. "This is Mr. Taylor, Mr. Burton, and Mr. Smith. Gentlemen, this is my daughter, Taisha." She peered over at them with wide eyes.

"It is very nice to meet you, Miss Taisha." Ian nodded to her regally.

"You talk funny," Taisha announced. All of the guys chuckled. "You're not from around here, are you?"

"No, Miss Taisha, we're not from around here." Ian leaned closer and told her in a stage whisper, "You talk funny as well."

"I do *not.*" Taisha drew her eyebrows together as she frowned, and turned back to Nathanial. "Can I stay the night at Jenny's or not?"

"What does your mother say?" Nathanial pulled her closer and lowered his face so they were eye level.

"She says to go ask my father," Taisha said, nodding.

"She did, did she?" Nathanial creased his eyebrows and cocked his head to the side as if he had to contemplate the situation. "Well, you can tell your mother…"

"What *exactly* can she tell her mother?" Monique came up behind him. Without missing a beat, Nathanial responded appropriately.

"You can tell your mother that if it's okay with *her*… it's okay with me."

"That's what I *thought*," Monique said.

Nathanial turned to his wife and regarded her tight lips and folded arms. *Uh oh… she's mad. What'd I do?*

"I already talked to Jenny's momma. We'll see you tomorrow morning." Although she spoke to Taisha while gently pulling her from Nathanial's arms, Monique didn't take her narrowed eyes off his. He gulped as he handed over their daughter, who ran off with her friend.

"Monique, I'd like you to meet…"

"I know who you are," Monique interrupted, turning her narrowed eyes on Ian. "I know why you're here, and no you are *not* stealing my husband away from his family and his church band."

"Uhh…" Ian shuffled his feet and the other guys sort of looked around the room. Just then,

Vanessa Ashton rushed up to Monique, carrying a baby in her arms.

"Monique, look at this adorable baby!" Vanessa drawled, holding the tiny boy out for Monique to take a peek under the little blue blanket. "Don't cha just want another one?"

Vanessa didn't seem to notice the tension in the group, but the two other ladies trailing behind Vanessa had wide eyes and raised brows. The woman with long, brown hair snuck up next to Ian and confidently met Monique's glare with a soft smile. The lady with long, blond curls stayed at Vanessa's shoulder. Nathanial assumed she must be the baby's mother.

Monique glanced at the baby and turned back to the group. Her stance was defiant—chin raised, arms crossed, feet planted. "You must be the world famous Megan..."

"It's very nice to meet you, Monique." Megan held out her hand. Monique hesitated before she pulled her arms apart and gripped Megan's outstretched hand.

"I have to admit, I loved that song Ian wrote for you." Monique glanced over at Ian dismissively and back to Megan. "What's it like? Being married to a rock star?"

"You tell me..." Megan challenged. "Your husband is one of the most talented drummers I've ever heard. Next to my husband of course."

"Of course…" Monique looked back up at Nathanial. He bit his lower lip and gave her his best puppy-dog eyes, pleading in his non-verbal way.

Could this really work? Could the two wives pull this together? If so, Nathanial would be forever grateful to Megan Taylor. It felt like everyone was holding their breath, especially Nathanial. He didn't dare speak. He couldn't imagine going against his wife's wishes. If only she could realize how important this was to him. If only she could understand this was his one shot at becoming a real musician, his one opportunity to be invited into a band with other extremely talented musicians, his one opportunity to play amongst equals. This was it. It all hinged on her.

Monique locked her eyes with his, defiantly at first, then considering, then softening, and finally relenting. Her countenance changed, and her shoulders dropped. Nathanial could see tears at the corners of her eyes, and her lower lip was shaking. *I'll find a way to make this work for our family,* Nathanial pleaded with his eyes. *You are still* the *most important thing in my life. I won't let you down! Please!*

"Fine…" Monique whispered. One tear ran down her cheek, and she turned to go.

"Monique." Megan put her hand on Monique's arm, but Monique yanked it away.

"Would you and Nathanial like to come get a bite to eat with all of us? I think we have a lot to discuss. Plus, I'd love to get to know you better. I hope we can become friends."

"I have plenty of friends right here at church and in my community." Monique crossed her arms again. "I don't need you people. I don't want my husband hangin' around you people. I know about what goes on when you go on those tours."

This isn't helping. This isn't helping. What do I do? Nathanial whipped his head around to meet Ian's concerned eyes. *Help!*

"Monique," Ian said. "I prayed about coming here to Nashville. I understand your concerns because I've had them, too. One of the reasons I feel so drawn to Nathanial is because of his strong values and commitment to God."

Monique's eyes met Ian's as a tear ran down each of her cheeks. "Or because you need a new drummer. That's the real reason you're here. Admit it."

"I *do* admit that." Ian shrugged. "I know people are brought in and out of our lives at the right time and in the right place. I would have never met Nathanial if I weren't looking for a new drummer, true. But I also would have never met him if he hadn't been performing in this worship service tonight."

"And," Andy interrupted. "I would have never met Nathanial if I hadn't met Vanessa at that café in London. They could all be coincidences."

"Or they could be part of a bigger plan." Ian shrugged. "A plan the likes of which we don't understand yet. All I know is that I feel drawn to this place, at this time, to meet this man… your husband."

"Come on, Monique," Vanessa begged. "Give it a chance. These people aren't bad."

"What happened to your purity ring, Vanessa?" Monique folded her arms across her chest again and looked pointedly down her nose at Vanessa.

"Uh…" Vanessa hesitated and glanced over at Andy.

"That's what I thought." Monique turned her glare on Nathanial. "See, *she's* already lowered her values after being around these people for just a few weeks. Is that what's going to happen to you? Are you going to be bombarded with women everywhere you go and wind up breaking our marriage vows in every town you play?"

"You know me better than that, Monique!" Nathanial held his hands up in defense. "We've been married for five years, and not once have my eyes ever strayed from you. My commitment to you is almost as strong as my commitment to God!"

"Yeah? Well, I would have thought Vanessa's commitment to God was stronger than that too!" Monique started toward him, pointing her finger at his chest. "Now she's fallen into Satan's trap by a man who seduced her while she was on vacation."

"I did no such thing," Andy held up his hands. "I never pressured her. She made her own choices."

"Oh yeah?" Monique turned on Andy. "Well, in case you need an anatomy and physiology lesson, a woman can't make *that* particular *choice* without a man's involvement. You could have *chosen* to respect her values."

"Oooo… she sounds like *you*, preacher boy." Kai nudged Ian with his elbow. "She could give you a run for your money preaching about the law of chastity."

"They call you preacher boy?" Nathanial snickered, glancing over at Ian. "You gonna steal my job as youth pastor?"

"You *are* going to need to post a help-wanted ad when we leave on tour." Ian crossed his arms and rubbed his chin. "Fill me in on your job description, and I'll let you know if I can handle the workload."

"Hey, if I'm going on tour, you're coming with me, so we're going to have to hire someone other than you," Nathanial reminded him.

"That's true." Ian winked at Nathanial.

"Job description?" Monique narrowed her eyes at Nathanial. "Want ad? Are you quitting your job as youth pastor?" Monique's voice rose.

How could she have not realized by now that I'd need to quit my job before going on tour? "Honey, I'll make more money playing in this band than I ever would as a youth pastor. We'll make ends meet, I promise."

"You'll be the richest man in your congregation," Ian mumbled.

"It is *not* about the money," Monique said. "And you *know* it. You're leaving your Christian band, and now you're leaving your church? What's next? You gonna leave me and Taisha? Oh… that's right! You *are!* You're leaving us behind while you run off with *these people*."

"It's not like that at all." Nathanial tried to think of a way to help her understand. "What if I had been a naval officer when you met me? Would you have tried to stop me from going overseas when I was called?"

"That's not the same thing," Monique said. "That's serving your country, not running off playing with a little rock band. Besides, I didn't marry a naval officer. I married a pastor." She folded her arms again and nodded definitively.

"You married a *seminary student* whose drum set was so big it barely fit into his tiny studio apartment," Nathanial reminded her. "You thought it was funny at the time."

Nathanial reached over and tried to tickle his wife. Monique pulled away, but not before he could see the little hint of a smile playing across her lips.

"You also liked it when I joined the Christian band because I moved the drum set out of our basement and over here to the church," Nathanial said. "What did you think was going to happen? That I would suddenly stop playing drums because I grew up?"

"I don't know..." Monique lifted her chin and her gaze to the far corner.

"Honey, I got news for you," Nathanial added. "You didn't marry a pastor who likes to play the drums. You married a drummer who happens to love the Lord and wants to serve God in all I do."

"Listen to us." Monique huffed. "We're already fighting and you haven't even signed a contract with them." Nathanial pulled her close and saw the little smile pulling at the corner of her mouth.

"I like fighting with you," Nathanial whispered close to her ear. "It always leads to makin' up later."

"You *stop*, Nathanial Jackson!" She tried to push him away, the smile growing wider and a sparkle gleaming in her eyes. "We are in mixed company… standin' in a church sanctuary no less. You're scandalous."

"Come on, sugar." Nathanial looked down into the most beautiful, chocolate eyes he'd ever seen. "Let's go have some dinner with our new friends so we can go home and make up." He planted a kiss on her cheek and released her gently from his arms.

"Scandalous…" She pushed him away. "I'm going to grab my jacket from the coat closet… Is it hot in here?"

Monique stepped down the stairs, and Nathanial turned back to his new band mates. They all seemed to be trying not to laugh.

"You're a sly dog, aren't you, Nathanial Jackson?" Ian pushed his shoulder lightly. "A scandalous, sly dog… but a really good drummer."

"Andy," Kai interrupted, raising his eyebrows suggestively. "I'd give a million pounds to go back in time and see the look on your face when you saw that purity ring for the first time."

"Shut up, Kai!" Andy grumbled.

"Guys, come here…" Ian pulled Nathanial closer, wrapped his arm around Kai's shoulders and raised his chin to Andy. He must have known exactly what Ian wanted because he looked up at Nathanial and reached his arm out as if he was going to give him a hug. Andy reached his other arm out and draped it around Kai's other shoulder. Nathanial looked down at Ian and realized his left arm was outstretched toward Nathanial just as Andy's was on his other side. *Group hug?* Nathanial raised his eyebrows at Ian, but Ian just tilted his head. "Come on…"

"Is this some kinda weird ritual y'all do?" Nathanial reluctantly stepped forward and wrapped his arms around a couple of skinny white guys' shoulders. It didn't feel *that* weird.

"Let's rock, on three. You ready?" Ian asked.

"Huh?"

"One, two, three…" Ian said.

"Let's rock," they said in unison.

Nathanial raised one eyebrow. "Uh… let's rock…"

"There ya go, mate!" Ian clapped him on the shoulder. "Let's rock!"

"Let's… rock," Nathanial repeated with a little more confidence. He nodded once and said with conviction, "Let's *rock.*"

CHAPTER THREE:
BASKETBALLS AND SNEAKERS

"Start over again! That's not right!" Ian ground his teeth together, trying not to raise his voice.

"Look, I know all of your songs, and I know how to *play* your songs," Nathanial said. "I don't need to take orders from a scrawny, little, white kid to know how to play *my* drums. You either want me in your band, or you don't. But I am *not* Gary Owens, and I'm going to do things *my* way. Is that clear, brotha'?" Their jam session in the recording studio was not going as planned.

Ian dug his fingernails into his palms and took a deep breath. *Scrawny? Kid? How dare he! This is my band. I give the orders.* Ian was used to getting his own way. It was true he was going to need to treat Nathanial differently than he had treated Gary, but he still had the upper hand in this bargain.

"I'll put it right back to you, mate," Ian said. "What else you going to do besides jam with us? Can you tour the world from the back of your little church band? I don't think so." Ian started to turn around, but Nathanial stood up from the stool behind his drum set and towered over him.

"I'm the youth pastor for the Nashville Church of Christ, and *the* drummer for the Christian band 'His Ministry.' I don't need to tour the world to feel *my* worth."

"Yeah, well your *worth* is going to have a lot greener bottom line if you stick with us, pal." Ian looked right up into his face, not afraid of Nathanial's challenge. "I'm sure your church could use a nice, new chapel. How would you like to be able to pull out your checkbook and *buy* them one?"

Nathanial narrowed his eyes. Ian could almost see the wheels turning behind Nathanial's expression. Living in inner city Nashville, he didn't have many opportunities to earn that kind of money. "We *could* use a new basketball gym for our youth program."

"*That* could be arranged." Ian narrowed his eyes right back.

"Fine, I'll stay." Nathanial sat down at the drums.

"Fine." Ian walked to the front of the group.

Kai and Andy looked at each other, failing miserably to conceal their grins.

"You got a problem, mates?" Ian looked back and forth between them. They just turned to the front and pretended to be tuning their guitars. This new dynamic was going to take some getting used to. Ian wasn't sure he could handle it.

* * * * * * * * *

"What am I supposed to do?" Ian pleaded with Kai. After twenty more minutes of tension and frustration, Kai had set his guitar in its stand and dragged Ian outside. "I don't understand what I'm doing *wrong?* Every time I tell him how the song is supposed to be played, he gets angry. I *know* how the songs are supposed to sound. I *wrote* the songs myself. Why doesn't he understand that?"

"Maybe because he hears them differently than you do." Kai reached out to Ian and put his hand on Ian's arm. "Or maybe he just doesn't like to be *told* what to do and how to do it."

Ian spoke through clenched teeth. "But they're *my* songs."

"They're *our* songs," Kai corrected him. "They're Buxton Peak's songs. And he's part of Buxton Peak now, so you're going to have to *find* a way to get along with him."

"I don't know how." Ian's face scrunched into a frown, and he crossed his arms. He knew he was acting immature, but he wasn't willing to relent.

"Maybe you should spend some time with him and get to know him."

"What do you think I've been *doing?*" Ian pointed in the direction of the recording studio in exasperation. "I spend every *day* with him, and we're getting nowhere."

"I meant outside of the recording studio," Kai said. "Away from me and Andy, and away from the pressures of music."

"What would you suggest?" Ian sneered, crossing his arms again. "That I take him out to lunch or something?"

"No, I mean get to know him on *his* turf." Kai turned Ian back around to look him in the eye. "Go volunteer at his youth program or something. Get to know Nathanial *the man*, not just Nathanial the drummer."

"Volunteer?"

"Think about it, Ian." Kai craned his neck down slightly to look Ian directly in the eye. "You, Andy, Gary, and I, we've known each other since we were kids. When you look at me a certain way, I know you heard that I was out of tune. When Andy is off time by a split second and you scrunch up your eyebrows, he fixes it.

And Gary, well, you and Gary had this weird connection that was almost creepy. It was like you were twins playing a set of drums simultaneously and either one of you could pick up the sticks and play the exact same rhythm without missing a beat. It was very strange."

Ian felt his mouth pull into a small grin, and he chuckled. Kai had a point.

"But Nathanial." Kai shook his head. "The two of you are not on the same wavelength yet. But you *could* be. You could really be something together. You both have more talent in your pinkie fingers than I have in my whole body. You could really jam... if *you*, Ian, can get yourself straightened out."

Ian looked up at Kai and nodded.

"Can you do that, mate?"

"Yeah, pal." Ian agreed. "I think I can do that."

"Well, get on with it then." Kai pushed Ian gently in the direction where he needed to go, literally and figuratively.

*   *   *   *   *   *   *   *   *

"I didn't know you had a piano here! I thought we were just coming to play basketball with the kids."

Nathanial sighed. He was going to have a

difficult time dragging Ian out of the common room and into the gym. Once Ian pulled out the little, wooden piano bench and opened the lid, exposing the keyboard, his eyes lit up and his fingers gracefully danced across the keys.

"Come on, brotha'," Nathanial said. "The teens are going to be here soon, and we got to get the gym opened and the heat turned on so they won't freeze."

"Whoa." Ian wrinkled his nose. "This piano is seriously out of tune. When was the last time you had it tuned?"

"I have no idea." Nathanial shook his head. "That's not in the budget."

"Don't you play it?" Ian dropped his jaw and looked up at him. "Can't you hear how bad it is?"

"No, I don't play the piano. I'm a *drummer*." Nathanial kept walking toward the gym. "Besides, like I said. It's not in the budget."

"Well, I'll pay for it then." Ian hurried to keep up. "You need a working piano in your youth center. That's just all there is to it."

"Look." Nathanial turned to Ian with a sneer. Ian almost ran right into him and looked up, with a bit of shock, at Nathanial towering above him. "You'd be hard-pressed to find a single one of these youth who even know *how* to play that thing, much less one who is interested in whether or not it's tuned. So don't waste your time or your money. If you have that much to spare, we have lots of other higher priorities you can throw money at."

"I have a *lot* of extra money to spare." Ian assured him with an innocence that made Nathanial shake his head in disbelief. This punk kid had no idea the kind of pressure this community was under financially. Tuning a piano? Ridiculous. He turned back around and kept walking, but Ian wasn't through. He pointed out the shabby furniture, the walls that needed painting and the floors that needed new carpeting. "We could fix this place up really nice."

"Put your money where your mouth is." Nathanial turned to him again. "Or shut up." Ian looked up at him with those same narrowed eyes and pulled his cell phone out of his pocket.

"Jeremy," Ian spoke into the receiver without breaking eye contact with Nathanial. "I need you to have someone come over to Nathanial's youth center and tune this piano for me."

Nathanial just narrowed his eyes right back and shook his head again. Ian had some nerve to come in here and start flashing around money for things that didn't matter.

"And I'm going to need a line of cash that I can draw from so I can help make some other changes around here. This place is in serious need of repairs and upgrades. Can you make those arrangements?" He listened for a moment, thanked his manager, and hung up the phone. Ian smirked right up at Nathanial. "*There*, now we have money. Let's go spend it on your youth program."

＊　＊　＊　＊　＊　＊　＊　＊　＊

"Woah! What's up with the skinny, white dude playing on our court?"

"Watch yourself, Tyrell," Nathanial said. "He's our guest. Is that the way we treat a guest?"

"Sorry, Pastor Nathan," Tyrell mumbled. He let his backpack fall off his shoulder and opened the zipper to remove a very worn, well-loved basketball.

"What's your problem, man?" Scott asked. "I'm white. You got beef with me, too?"

"Nah, man, you're swole!" Tyrell shoved his friend's shoulder. "I don't care what color your skin is, as long as you can dunk over East High's center."

"I can dunk over you!" Scott knocked the ball out of Tyrell's hands, dribbled it across the court, took three steps for a layup, and shoved the ball through the hoop, where he hung from the rim with one hand.

"Sweet!" Tyrell rebounded the ball and shot

from the three-point line, easily sliding the ball through hoop. "Nothin' but net!"

"And the crowd goes wild!" Ian called from behind the boys. They both turned around and looked Ian up and down. "What's the matter? Old-fashioned joke?"

"If that's what you wanna call yo'self," Scott said.

"Scott Sanborn! Where are your manners?" Nathanial scolded him.

"Sorry, Pastor Nathan." Scott mumbled under his breath, "He knew I was joking."

"I'm sure he did," Nathanial said. "It's still not polite."

"Why's he here, anyway?" Tyrell had retrieved his basketball and was rolling it between his hands.

"Bro," Scott said, pushing Tyrell's shoulder. "That's Ian *Taylor!*"

"How about if we start speaking *to* Mister Taylor, since he's right here in the room, rather than speaking *about* him?" Nathanial suggested.

Tyrell palmed the basketball in his left hand and reached over with his right hand to introduce himself. "Hello, Mr. Taylor. I'm Tyrell Gibbons. It's nice to meet you."

"It's nice to meet you as well." Ian shook Tyrell's hand. "I'm Ian Taylor, as your mate pointed out."

"Are you famous or something?" Tyrell stepped back and bounce passed the ball to Ian, who caught the ball and held it in both hands.

"Dude, he's from that rock band who's stealing Pastor Nathan from us," Scott said.

"Why do they keep calling you Pastor Nathan?" Ian stage whispered to Nathanial. "Don't they like your *regular* name?"

"It's cumbersome," Nathanial explained.

"Okay then, Pastor Nathan it is." Ian held the basketball up. "Who's up for some hoops? I know I wouldn't be your top choice for a teammate, but we could play some two-on-two until some other guys get here."

The door slammed open and two more teen boys entered ahead of three teen girls. Suddenly there was enough people for three-on-three and a cheering section.

"Oh my gosh!" one of the girls squealed. "Ian Taylor is here!"

"Why is it you cause problems everywhere you go?" Nathanial asked Ian.

"I honestly don't mean to," Ian said. "I just don't get it. I'm no different than any other guy."

"Yeah, right," Nathanial mumbled. "Okay, bring it in; let's have a little chat." All the teens gathered around, and two of the girls giggled. Samantha even sidled up next to Ian. Nathanial narrowed his eyes at her, and she took one step away.

Little Mary, who looked way too young to be a senior in high school, casually stepped around the back of the group to stand next to Tyrell. They didn't even look at one another, or hold hands, or anything, but there was something there. *Hmm… when did that start?*

"Okay," Nathanial said, returning to the task at hand. "As most of you have probably heard, the rock band, Buxton Peak has asked me to join them as their new drummer. I'm not resigning from my job as your pastor… yet."

There were murmurs throughout the group of teens, some excited faces, some forlorn, Tyrell even had his brow furrowed as if this news was a shock. *He hadn't heard?* Nathanial took a deep breath.

"It won't be for a while." Nathanial held up his hands to calm them down. "I promise we'll find someone good to replace me, but I'll eventually be going on tour with the band."

Samantha leaned closer to Ian as if she were interested in hearing more about his tour. She even batted her eyelashes and smiled at him. *I don't think so!* Nathanial pushed casually in between the teenage girl and Ian, shoving her aside with a warning look, and draped his arm around Ian's shoulders.

"Since we're staying here in Nashville

rehearsing, Mr. Taylor and his *wife* Megan," Nathanial looked pointedly down at Samantha, "are going to be helping fix up the youth center. He wants to get some new furniture and new carpet and paint the walls, and he even wants to fix up that *old* piano."

"I didn't know we had a piano." Allie, one of the younger girls wrinkled her nose and cocked her head.

"It's right next to the television," Samantha reminded her. "With the bench that we use to reach the DVDs on the top shelf."

"Oh yeah…"

"Do any of you know how to play?" Ian sounded more hopeful than doubting.

"My grandma taught me a few things when I was younger," Mary shrugged. "I think if I'd kept up with it, I might have been kind of good."

"That's really cool." Ian nodded. "I'm going to get it tuned and maybe we can find some sheet music. I'll bet we could get some lessons for some of you, if you want."

"Would *you* be the one teaching the lessons?" Samantha batted her eyelashes at him. She lowered her gaze when she noticed Nathanial's piercing glare.

"No," Ian reminded her. "Pastor Nathan and I will be heading off on tour in a few months, but we'll make some arrangements to have someone come in to teach you."

"I think I'd like to learn again," Mary said. "That would be fun. And, thank you Mister Taylor for helping fix up the youth center. We really appreciate it. Don't we, guys?" She turned to the other teens in the group, and they nodded enthusiastically or shuffled their feet or mumbled 'thanks.' *Always the leader.* Nathanial nodded to her. *Nice job.*

"You're welcome." Ian rolled the ball in his hands, gulped, and changed the subject. "I'm starving. Do you have any food around here, or should I order a bunch of pizzas?"

"Pizza!" There was a general consensus.

"Where do you normally order pizza from?" Ian requested, pulling out his cell phone. They all looked at him with shocked stares, and some even shook their heads. "Let me guess, that's not in the budget?"

"You got it, brotha'." Nathanial patted him on the shoulder.

"We're going to have to get you a bigger budget," Ian suggested. The kids all looked at him with round eyes and apprehension. "What other kinds of things do you need? Some new basketballs? Bigger television? Maybe a video game system?"

"I need some new kicks," Scott quietly suggested. Quite a few of them nodded, and they all looked down at their feet. Several of the kids had very worn-out sneakers, some were even held together with duct tape. For a few minutes, things got awkward as the kids compared holes and general wear & tear of one another's shoes.

"Well, I think some new sneakers should be *second* on our list then." Ian smiled and clapped his hands. Eyebrows went up, smiles crept onto faces, and disbelief reigned among the group's countenance. "But pizza first. You got a phone book around here? Ah, stupid question. Okay Google… where's the closest pizza delivery?"

CHAPTER FOUR:
NO HOLDING BACK

"Megan," Ian whispered in the dark. He was keenly aware she was still awake. "They have *nothing*. Their shoes are falling apart and the carpets are threadbare. They have to leave the heat off during the day because they can't afford to have it on when they're not in the building. We have to *do* something."

"What would you suggest?" Megan rolled over and peered at him through the darkened bedroom.

"Well, I need to get them some new sneakers immediately," Ian said. "Then maybe we'll plan a work day where we have the kids help rip up the old carpet and scrape the old paint and pick out their own paint colors, and really take ownership of the project, you know?"

"It sounds like you're on the right track," Megan said. "Just make sure you don't spend too much on the shoes."

"Why?" Ian pushed himself up on his elbow to look down at her. "Don't they deserve to have nice things?"

"In that neighborhood, expensive shoes would get stolen right off their feet. Things are different in big cities. You and I have lived sheltered lives in rural communities where you can literally walk out to your back yard and pick food from the ground. These kids don't have that. If one of them has more than the others, it becomes a source of contention and jealousy."

"I've traveled all over the world. I've been in plenty of big cities and no one has beaten me up and stolen my shoes."

"Have you ever walked through a big city *without* a bodyguard?" Megan raised her eyebrows. He sighed, knowing she was right. He'd been spoiled most of his life and had taken many things for granted. "Just get them something simple and high quality, but normal, everyday shoes. Nothing fancy."

"All right." He sighed and lay back down on his pillow. He put his hands behind his head and looked up at the ceiling. "The kids want to meet you, by the way. Will you come to the youth center with me tomorrow?"

"Sure, and I'll bring some shoe samples with me."

"Why do you need shoe samples?" Ian creased his forehead as he turned on his pillow.

"So they can pick them out and try them on," Megan explained. "I'll have Vanessa & Rhonda help me go buy a few pairs in a variety of sizes, and we can have the kids try them on, and we'll write down exactly what size & styles they each want and get them ordered."

"See, *that's* why I married you." Ian pulled her close. "You're so smart. I never would have thought of that."

"I thought you just married me so you could sleep with me…"

"You know me too well." Ian grinned at her. "But in all seriousness, you are really smart, and I don't know what I'd do without you."

"You're not going to start crying, are you?" Megan teased him.

"Men don't cry."

"Yeah, right." She laughed. "Get over here and kiss me you sappy, old man."

"Old?" He feigned offense. "The other day Nathanial called me a scrawny kid, and now you're calling me old? I sure *feel* old today after playing basketball with a bunch of teenagers."

"Gee, if you're too tired…" She started to turn away from him.

"I'm never too tired for *that*." He pulled her back into his arms. "Get over here, woman. You said you wanted a kiss from a sappy, old man. Don't deny me now."

"Never…"

* * * * * * * * *

"It was good of you to come yesterday…" Nathanial hesitated. "I'm sorry I was rude."

"It's me who should be apologizing." Ian stopped him. "I know I can be a jerk sometimes, but I'm trying to change. I hope you'll put up with me for a bit longer. I can learn a lot from you." Ian stuck out his hand in truce, waiting for Nathanial to meet him halfway. They shook hands and nodded, looking one another in the eye.

"Likewise," Nathanial said.

"I asked Andy and Kai to stay home today," Ian said. "I want you to have the studio to yourself. I'm going to walk into the sound room, and you're going to be alone with your drum set."

"But…" Nathanial interrupted.

"Hear me out, mate." Ian held out a hand. "I'm going to turn on the tracks of Kai's guitar, Andy's bass, and my vocals, and we're going to put a microphone in front of you in case you want to add your own vocals to the songs, and I want you to wail on those drums and play the songs the way *you* think they should be played. I don't want you to see my facial expressions; I don't want to offer my insight in any way. I want you to play the songs the way you *hear* them. No holding back. I want you to play as if no one's watching. I'm going to record you, and then I'm going to take those recordings home and listen to them over and over and over until they sound right to *me*."

"You're not kidding?"

"I'm not kidding." Ian raised his eyebrows. "You are one of the most talented drummers I've ever heard, and you need a chance to play with your whole soul, maybe for the first time in your life, at least in a recording studio anyway."

Nathanial smiled and nodded before breaking out into a full grin. "This is gonna be fun." He walked back to his drum set and sat down.

"I'm going to play every song Buxton Peak has ever recorded, starting with the ones we'd like to play on our next tour." Ian explained. "You tell me if you want me to start a track over, or if you need a break, or if you need to be done for the day."

By this time Nathanial was laughing and smiling and fiddling with his sticks, anxious to get started.

"I've even arranged for your other pastor to

handle the youth program today," Ian said. "Megan, Vanessa, Rhonda, and Monique are helping the teens try on their new shoes so we can get them ordered. They're also bringing some paint swatches and fabric and all kinds of other things for them to start picking out and planning what their new youth center is going to look like."

"That's awesome, brotha'." Nathanial twirled the drumstick in his right hand. "Let's rock!"

"Let's rock." Ian grinned at him and walked out the door. He sat down in the sound room, turned on the first track, and let the magic happen.

* * * * * * * * *

"What'ch you two doin' in here?" Nathanial asked. Mary and Tyrell startled and let go of each other's hands. They inched farther away from each other, but were a little too close prior to Nathanial walking into the common room.

"Just studyin' Pastor Nathan." Tyrell turned on his seat, back toward his notebooks and grabbed a pencil. Mary lowered her eyes and picked at her fingernails. "Mary's been tutoring me to help me get my grades up. Still hopin' for that scholarship."

"Is that so…" Nathanial sat at the table across

from them, his large frame straining the cheap wooden seat. "What class are you studying for?"

"Math," Tyrell said.

"Chemistry," Mary spoke at the same time. Their wide eyes met, and Mary gulped.

"What I mean is," Tyrell corrected. "There are so many equations in chemistry, that it *feels* like we're studying math."

"Yeah, I think there's a little more *chemistry* going on in this room than studying, am I right?" Nathanial pursed his lips and looked pointedly at one and then the other. Although the common room at the youth center was an open area, Nathanial could tell there was more than just studying going on, and it involved roaming hands and subtle innuendos.

"Well, you know…" Tyrell tried unsuccessfully to hide a smile playing at the corners of his mouth. "Chemistry's my favorite subject." Mary snickered and covered her mouth to hide her laugh.

Nathanial turned around and reached behind him to a shelf where he knew there was a stack of Bibles. "Let's study a little more about chemistry, shall we?" He began flipping pages.

Both teenagers faced forward with stoic faces. Tyrell cleared his throat, reached into his backpack for a cover-worn Bible, and opened the book, waiting for a reference. This was a common occurrence at the youth center. Whenever Nathanial had a point to make, they all knew he was inevitably going to turn to God's word.

"Mary, how about if you start us out," Nathanial said.

"Me?" She put her hand to her heart and blinked her eyes. "Wh... where?"

"Turn to second Corinthians, chapter seven." Nathanial began flipping pages. "Read verse fifteen for us."

"Uh, okay." Mary gulped and leaned over Tyrell's shoulder. He pushed the Bible a little closer to her and winked. "And his inward affection is more abundant toward you, whilst he remembereth the obedience of you all, how with fear and trembling ye received him." Mary stopped and glanced up at Tyrell with wide eyes.

"Now, Tyrell, you read Proverbs chapter six verse twenty-five," Nathanial said. Tyrell cleared his throat and pulled the Bible back from Mary.

"Lust not after her beauty in thine heart..." Tyrell stopped and held up his hands in resignation. "Okay, okay, I think we get your point. So we like each other. There's no crime in that."

"Whosoever looketh on a woman to lust after her," Nathanial started. Tyrell joined in while rolling his eyes.

"Hath committed adultery with her already in his heart." Tyrell took a deep breath. "I'm very familiar with the verse."

"Matthew five, twenty-eight," they said together.

"I know, I know…"

"I know that you know, and that's why I want you to be careful," Nathanial told them. "You two have your whole lives ahead of you, and there's time for all that jazz later on… when you're older… and married."

"What are we studying?" A voice from behind them called out. Ian and Megan walked into the common room of the youth center, holding hands.

"Chemistry," Nathanial, Tyrell, and Mary all said at the same time. Nathanial felt as sheepish as the kids looked.

Megan sat next to Mary, bumping her shoulder. The two had connected on the day everyone tried on shoes. Nathanial heard the following day that Mary had been very helpful and a true leader to the younger kids.

"The guy is coming to tune the piano today," Ian said, sitting next to Nathanial. I thought we'd come over and watch."

"Will you play us a song afterward?" Mary batted her eyelashes and smiled at Ian. She was shy and timid, not flirting with Ian like some of the other girls.

"What song would you like me to play?" Ian pulled the Bible closer to him and flipped through pages.

"Do you know *Rock of Ages?*" Mary raised her eyebrows, fidgeting with the corner of the worn leather on the Bible that still sat halfway between her and Tyrell.

"That's one of my favorite hymns!" Ian got up from the table, pulled out the piano bench and lifted the fallboard from the keys. His fingers immediately danced across the keys before he wrinkled his nose and pushed himself away. "How about if I wait until *after* it's been tuned?"

"Could you maybe play that love song you wrote for your wife?" Tyrell glanced over at Megan.

"*Passing through Eternity?*" Ian asked. "You've listened to my music."

"Yeah, kinda…" Tyrell said, pursing his lips and looking away.

"I love that song…" Mary whispered under her breath. "It's *so* romantic."

A man with a workbag stepped tentatively through the door. "Is this where the piano needs to be tuned?" Ian stood up and met the guy halfway across the room, shaking his hand and inviting him toward the piano.

Tyrell took the distraction to close his Bible

and wink at Mary. Nathanial couldn't decide what to do about those two. They were such good kids, quoting scriptures and requesting their favorite hymns to be played by a rock star known for pounding beats and screaming guitars. But there was an underlying tension between the two of them. *God, help me counsel these young ones. They are already way over the line…*

CHAPTER FIVE:
WELCOME 'HOME'

"Well, it's about time." Ian held open the door to his new home, which was more like a mansion sitting aloft an expansive estate. "Welcome home, mate!"

"I'm not staying." Ed stepped through the doorway, but his distant stare wasn't admiring the beautiful entryway. "I need to go back to Michigan."

"You just got here..." Ian felt his heart grow heavy. "You're not resigning as my bodyguard, are you?"

"I'm not sure." Ed pushed past Ian and invited himself down the hall and into the kitchen, where he held open the refrigerator door but stared at the contents within, not reaching for food. Finally he pulled out a water bottle and opened it without speaking. His brows creased as he downed half the bottle and sighed.

"Are you hungry, pal?" Ian slid past Ed to the fridge for a leftover casserole from the night before. Without asking if Ed wanted any, Ian got out a microwave dish and scooped up a generous helping, not turning around again until he pulled the steaming plate out and handed it to Ed, along with a fork.

Ed scooped forkfuls of chicken and broccoli into his mouth, but didn't seem to even register he was eating, much less enjoying it. He just stood there, staring out the window as he ate. Ian fixed himself a plate and sat at the kitchen island, slowly eating and observing.

"What's wrong, Ed?" Ian forked a bite into his mouth, concerned for his friend.

"I can't leave her there…" Ed's wide-eyed, blank expression drew Ian's attention out the kitchen window to the beautiful gardens. Ian hadn't even had a chance to explore them. They'd just moved in a few days prior, and he'd barely started unpacking, much less wandering outside. He put his hand on Ed's sleeve, pulling his attention back inside.

"Who? India?" Ian cocked his head. "Why didn't she come with you?"

"I didn't ask her to come with me…"

"Why not?" Ian scratched his head.

"Where would she live?" Ed asked. "I don't even know where I'm going to live." Ed glanced around the expansive kitchen with a panicked expression.

"For now you're going to stay with us, right?" Ian asked.

"I guess." Ed sat down hard on one of the chairs. "I hadn't thought that far ahead. You sent me a plane ticket. I got on the plane."

"What did India say?" Ian scooted his chair closer to Ed. "You've been dating for over a year now, right? Don't you think it's time you make some decisions about your future?"

"She's furious, of course. She said I care more about you than I do about her."

"Is that true?" Ian leaned forward, trying to get Ed to look him in the eye.

"Is what true?" Ed's eyes met Ian's, still confused.

"Do you care about me more than you care about her?" Ian asked.

"What kind of a stupid question is that?" Ed creased his forehead. "You're my best mate… but I'm in *love* with her."

"Does she know you're in love with her?" Ian raised his eyebrows.

"Well, she should." Ed's face pulled together in a scowl. "We've been dating for over a year."

"Have you ever *told* her you love her?" Ian

asked.

"N… no… shouldn't she just know that?"

"You've never told her you loved her?" Ian's jaw dropped. "And you think she should just *know* you love her?"

"She's never told me she loves me." Ed pouted and shrugged.

"Guys are supposed to say 'I love you' first, you dork!" Ian reached over and smacked Ed on the back of his head. *"Do* you love her?"

"Of course I love her!"

"What are your intentions with this girl?" Ian asked.

"She's not a girl…" Ed's expression changed to a cheesy, far-off look. "She's a *woman."* Ed sighed, and Ian lost his temper.

"Get your sorry rear end to Michigan and don't come back to Nashville until she's Mrs. Williams!" Ian said.

"Really?" A smile spread across Ed's face.

Ian shook his head and pulled out his cell phone. He hit the button for the first person on his contacts list. "Jeremy, I need you to get a plane ticket to take Ed back to Michigan immediately. Can you make that arrangement?"

Ian waited for his manager to respond, then pulled the phone away from his ear, and gaped at Ed.

"Why are you still sitting in my kitchen? Get to

the airport... now!"

Ed jumped out of his seat and ran from the room. Ian shook his head with an amused grin and pulled the phone back to his ear.

"When are *you* coming to Nashville?" Ian asked Jeremy.

"I wanted to make sure Gary was settled with his mother before I left England," Jeremy answered. "He just got out of rehab and honestly doesn't look all that great. I don't have a lot of confidence in his full recovery."

"So are you staying in Manchester then?" Ian asked.

"I'm not his babysitter," Jeremy said. "I'm Buxton Peak's manager. You need me in Nashville if we're ever going to get back on tour."

"I certainly can't do it without you," Ian said. "I'm just the singer and songwriter, after all."

"Yeah, right. Sell that lie to someone else. How's our new drummer working out?"

"Nathanial and I had our disagreements in the beginning, but we're getting along famously now."

"Does he realize how famous he's about to become?" Jeremy asked.

"Probably not, but don't frighten him before we even get him onstage," Ian said. "Hey, I'm keeping you from making the arrangements to help Ed. He's going to be at the airport before we even get off the phone if we're not careful. Let me know when you get to Nashville. We have plenty of space here while you get settled."

"See you soon, Ian."

"Bye, Jeremy."

CHAPTER SIX:
AND THE WINNER IS...

"How long ago did you guys win New Artist of the Year at the American Music Awards?" Jeremy mused, as if he didn't already know the exact date and time. He was sauntering across the practice room as if bored.

"Six years ago last November." Ian strummed a chord on an acoustic guitar, mostly ignoring his manager.

"And Best Rock Group at the Teen Choice Awards?"

"Five years ago in August, why?" Ian narrowed his eyes. *Where's he going with this?*

"How about Top Hot 100 Song?" Jeremy raised his eyebrows up and down. That stopped Ian short. The only time they'd gone to the Billboards was when they won Top Rock Album three years ago. That could only mean one thing.

"*Passing Through Eternity* has been nominated for best song... of the *whole* year?"

"*That* is correct!" Jeremy laughed. "You're going to the Billboard Music Awards."

"Do the other guys know?" Ian asked.

"I wanted to tell you first, since you wrote the song. Plus I have a question for you." Jeremy hesitated. "How would you feel about inviting Gary to the awards show?"

"That would be great," Ian said. "Do you know where he is?"

"I'm working on it." Jeremy pulled up a chair, turned it around and sat down, leaning against the back and resting his arms on the top.

"I just have one condition," Ian said. "I want Nathanial with us as well. He's part of Buxton Peak now. I'm not excluding him just because Gary was there at the time the song was written and originally performed."

"I think that's fair," Jeremy acknowledged. "They also want to know if you'd like to perform that night."

"I don't think we're ready for that yet." Ian shook his head. "We haven't even announced our next tour dates, we're not done learning the sets, and I don't want there to be an awkward moment where we kick Gary off the stage so that Nathanial can play with us. No, it's not time yet."

"I agree." Jeremy nodded. "We'll leave it at that. All five of you will sit in the audience together, and then *if* you win, you'll all go up there as a group."

"That sounds like a plan." Ian confirmed. "Maybe we should announce our tour dates between now and then, and that night we can officially introduce Nathanial to the world. We've been rehearsing openly for weeks, but we've never held a press conference or anything."

"I think that can be arranged. I'll get to work on finalizing plans for tour dates, and I'll let the producers know. This is going to be exciting."

"Next phase in our careers are about to begin, mate." Ian smiled. "Did you ever guess we'd take it this far?"

"Honestly…" Jeremy started to shake his head, but nodded wholeheartedly. "Yes, I did. The first time I saw you I knew there was something special about you. When I heard you play, I was ready to sign you immediately. When you pulled that crazy stunt of leaving all of us for two years, I thought you were daft out of your mind until I heard you speak in church, and I just *knew* that God was going to bless you for your dedication, sacrifice, and commitment. I just knew it. That's when I knew we were going all the way together. It was like God spoke to my heart and gave me peace that day."

"That's really deep, mate. Why didn't you ever tell me that?"

"It would have gone to your head." Jeremy laughed. "You were such a cocky little thing back then. Still are sometimes."

"Why does everybody wanna call me little?" Ian pouted. "I'm not that little."

"Comparatively…" Nathanial boomed from behind him. Ian hadn't realized the rest of the band had begun shuffling into the studio ready to warm up. "Yes, you are."

"Thanks, pal." Ian frowned.

"Anytime, brotha'." Nathanial slapped him on the back playfully.

*　*　*　*　*　*　*　*　*

"And the winner is…" The young actress hesitated for dramatic effect. Then she and her co-presenter announced together, "*Passing through Eternity* by Buxton Peak!" The audience rose to its feet in celebration and the television cameras panned to the section of the auditorium where the entire entourage sat together with wives, girlfriends, bodyguards, and their manager. Each of the guys hugged his girl and high-fived or fist-bumped one another, and then the five band members of Buxton Peak headed up to the stage. It was a strange assortment of characters.

Ian felt bad for Gary. His former band, together with their *new* drummer, was winning an award for a song Gary didn't help write, would never perform again, and wasn't sober enough to remember anyway. He played along. He smiled when he was supposed to smile, climbed the stairs right along with everyone else as if it was a normal day. But it was strained. It was all very strained.

Nathanial looked as if he was gritting his teeth. He and Gary had a tense moment when meeting for the first time, sat on opposite ends of the group, and now stood on opposite ends of the stage. Neither of them looked happy.

Ian took to the microphone first, but had to wait for at least a minute for the audience to calm down and the girls in the balcony to finish screaming. When it was finally almost quiet, one last girl called out, "We love you!" and that was the first issue Ian addressed when he spoke.

"We love you too!" he called and then had to wait again while the crowd roared. Finally things calmed down, and he began again. "Seriously though, you are the best fans *ever*, and we wouldn't be where we are today without your support."

More screaming, more applause, more smiles. Then Ian got down to a little more business and addressed the obvious.

"As I'm sure you're aware, Buxton Peak has made some changes in recent months." He stopped and grinned over at Nathanial. "We have an extra mate here with us now. I'd like to introduce our new drummer, Nathanial Jackson."

The crowd applauded and squealed with excitement and anticipation. Nathanial didn't seem entirely ready for the unearned fame of *being* in Buxton Peak, but he waved and smiled.

"I want to let you know that our mate Gary Owens will be taking a little break from our crew." Ian pulled Gary over, and they draped arms over one another's shoulders as the crowd booed. Gary waved just a little, similar to how Nathanial had done. "We've been together since we were teenagers in Derbyshire, and we're going to miss him, but we wish him the best of luck."

With that, Ian pulled away from Gary and led the applause, and then Ian stepped back to allow Gary time at the microphone. Gary didn't step up to speak, just waved out to the crowd as they applauded and screamed for him. After a few awkward seconds, Kai stepped up to the microphone to offer some traditional acknowledgements, thanking their manager Jeremy, their families and friends and fans, record label, and producers. Ian came back to the microphone and said what everyone was waiting to hear.

"I would be remiss not to offer appreciation and love for the woman who inspired our song, my wife, Megan." Ian looked down at her, and they smiled at one another. She even blew him a little kiss from across the way, and the crowd loved it. The fans in the balcony chanted her name the same way they had at the concert in Copenhagen, and Megan stood, turned around, and waved at them. That drew more applause as she sat down. Ian closed out his comments with one more cliché but expected recognition. "Most importantly, I have to give all the credit to God, without whom none of this would be possible. After all, it is His eternity that we are all just passing through."

That brought another thunderous applause and the five guys stood side by side with arms around each others' shoulders one last time before walking off the stage together. That was the first and last time Buxton Peak was complete.

* * * * * * * * *

"How are you feeling… really?" Ian poked Gary on the leg, urging him to meet Ian's gaze. "Don't lie to me."

"I'm fine." Gary's eyes shifted somewhere off Ian's shoulder, and he folded his arms across his chest. There wasn't much to look at in the small dressing room.

"You're stoned," Ian said. "I'm not stupid."

"How is that different than any time you've seen me in the last few years? I'm fine." Gary had taken a sudden interest in the pattern on the sofa cushion. The room was surprisingly quiet considering how many people were still backstage at the awards show. Ian was glad to have a few minutes alone with Gary. It had been too long since they'd seen each other, and they hadn't left on good terms.

"What happened to getting help?" Ian asked.

"I don't need any help." Gary's hard eyes focused on Ian as best as he was capable.

"You know I'm here for you, right? You can talk to me, pal."

"No, Ian. You're *not* here for me. You've moved on, and I'm done with all of it. The band, the travelling, the fighting, I'm done. We had a fun go of it, but it's over. Buxton Peak is over."

Buxton Peak is not over, Ian sat back and folded his arms, glad he hadn't voiced his opinion out loud. But Gary was right about one thing. He was done. Ian had known it for a long time, but this conversation cemented the decision. Gary Smith was no longer a member of Buxton Peak. *But you'll always be one of my best mates. How can I help you see that?* Ian's throat tightened. He forced out a whisper. "What are you planning to do now?"

"Go back to Manchester." Gary said it as if he was stating the obvious. "I wanna go home. I want to rest. I want to drive up onto the Peaks and stare up into the grey sky and do nothing."

Ian could picture Gary doing just that. His glazed eyes painted that vision of Gary's current reality. He wasn't living on the same plane where Ian was. He was too far gone. Ian couldn't help it this time; a tear escaped down the side of his cheek, and he turned away. His whisper was barely audible, even to himself. "I love you, Gary."

"I love you too, pal." Gary stood up, put his hand on Ian's shoulder, and walked from the room.

* * * * * * * * *

"What's all this?" Monique pushed open the door to the backstage holding room along with Vanessa, Rhonda, and finally Megan. Ian's heart raced as he suddenly realized how this must look.

An all-girl singing group of four very nice-looking ladies was sitting casually with an all-guy rock band in a small, private room, discussing the possibility of going on tour with them. Buxton Peak had yet to decide who'd open for them on their first tour in over a year, and someone suggested they consider these relatively new performers. The two groups met backstage at the awards show to see if they'd be a good fit and were sitting around laughing and talking when the wives and girlfriends walked in together.

All conversation stopped and proverbial daggers flew between the two sets of women. The committed relationships versus the potential mistresses.

The situation reminded Ian why the phrase "avoid the appearance of evil" was so important. Ian and Nathanial were the first two to hop off their chairs and rush to their wives' sides. It was actually quite telling about the higher level of commitment that existed between a husband and wife rather than just a live-in boyfriend and girlfriend.

Andy was the next to hurry to Vanessa's side, but Ian actually saw a slight spark fly between Kai and one of the girls. Still, he strode over to Rhonda and held out his arm as if to remind her that *she* was the woman who would be on his arm for the remainder of the evening and the one with whom he would go home.

"I knew this was going to happen." Monique shoved Nathanial away and folded her arms across her chest, pinching her lips together.

"Well, I can see the party's over," one of the female singers mumbled. The four girls rose from their seats and made their way toward the door.

They smiled coyly at the guys, and the one winked at Kai as she sashayed by. The lead singer turned back. "Let us know what you decide."

"I've already decided," Ian said, shaking his head. "I don't think it's a good idea. Good luck to you ladies." He tried to sound insistent and dismissive, leaving no doubt in anyone's minds.

Ian turned around to find four women glaring at him. He raised his eyebrows. "Don't worry, it's not happening. We'll find a nice, fledgling rock band of talented *guys* to open for us."

"Don't worry?" Megan's lip shook, and a hint of moisture was in her eyes. But what caught Ian's attention was the hardness in her expression. Anger mixed with sadness mixed with betrayal. "Wouldn't you worry? If you walked into a tiny room to find us surrounded by guys who were looking at us like they wanted to rip our clothes off and take advantage of us?"

"They weren't doing that." Ian tried to laugh off the situation, but realized Megan's assessment wasn't far from the truth. Since his early teens, girls had been looking at him that way. It usually didn't bother him because he knew it would never go beyond that, but Andy, Gary, and especially Kai had too frequently took advantage of these exact situations. This would be the first tour where they were in committed relationships, and the flirting had to stop.

"Yeah, they were," Megan said, stomping off in the direction of Ian's personal dressing room. Ian quickly followed. He closed the door behind them, afraid she'd slam it if given the chance. She turned to him with vitriol in her eyes. "You flirt with women all the time. I've never said anything to you about it, because it's just your personality, but I don't think you fully realize the way you affect girls when you do that. It confuses them and makes them think they stand some fighting chance with you."

"Well, they don't," Ian said. "You, of all people, should know that."

"I also think it kind of excites you." Her voice lowered in frustration.

"What?" Ian creased his eyebrows. "What do you think? That I flirt with other women and come home and make love to my wife? Is that what you think?"

"You said it, not me." She shrugged and folded her arms across her chest.

"Maybe you're right," Ian admitted. Megan's head snapped up. "My personality is very flirtatious. The guys told me that a long time ago. They also told me I shouldn't change a thing about myself because that's just the way I am. My personality is what has gotten us this far."

"That's not exactly fair to me, is it?" Megan sat on the arm of the sofa.

"You liked my flirtatious personality when we first met, admit it." He came over and brushed a stray hair from her forehead.

"That's when I thought you were only flirting with me," Megan said. "I never realized you were flirting with hundreds of girls. You could have a girl in every city you travel. I know it by the way they look at you. All you guys would've had to do tonight was reach out and lock that door and none of us girls would have known a thing."

"You're right." Ian raised his eyebrows, challenging her right back. "And did we?"

"No…" Megan whispered. She picked a piece of lint from her vintage cocktail dress. Ian reached out and tilted her chin with one finger. Her beautiful hazel eyes shone in the soft light of the dressing room.

"I have *never* locked the door to my dressing room," Ian said. "Believe me; I've had *thousands* of chances. Do you know how many girls I've kissed in my lifetime?"

Megan gulped. "I'm afraid to ask."

"Three…" Ian raised his eyebrows, and Megan's jaw dropped. "A cute little redhead in high school, who *believe* me, wanted more than a kiss. A semi-serious relationship after my mission… and the most beautiful woman in the world… you."

"I'm *not* the most beautiful woman in the

world," Megan said. "I'm not glamorous or exciting or fun. There's nothing remotely sexy about me… I can understand why you'd think about other women when you're stuck with me."

"Look at me, Megan." Ian lifted her from the arm of the sofa, but didn't pull her into his arms. He scooted her over so she was sitting on the cushions and knelt in front of her. "I am not *stuck* with you. I *chose* you. And *you* chose *me*. Am I right?"

"Yeah…" Megan reached up and ran her fingers through his hair. Ian shivered. Nothing in the world felt as good as when she touched him. He forced himself to focus.

"God brought us together because we were meant to be together," Ian whispered. "I don't *see* anyone else but you. You are everything to me. You have been since the first time I saw you from across the room and knew *who* you were. Instinctively. You are the woman God made for me. And I am the man God made for you. Not because you're beautiful or exciting or sexy, which you *are* by the way."

He ran his hands along the outside of her legs, loving the chiffon dress that draped across her lap. Her breathing increased, and passion entered her expression.

"I love you because you are my eternal companion." Ian's hands wrapped around her waist firmly. "Our marriage is forever, and our love is forever. You're everything to me."

"Ian, you're everything to me, too." Megan whispered. She rested her hands on his forearms and squeezed gently. "I knew it the day we met. I just fought it because I felt so inferior. I mean, look at you. You're drop-dead handsome with an amazing voice and eyes that make me melt. You captured my heart the minute you started talking to me. You looked at me as if you already knew me and already loved me before we met."

"I did," he reminded her. "I've loved you forever. And you know what else? My hair is going to fall out someday, and I'm probably going to get fat and lazy, and I might even lose my singing voice and be old and wrinkly. Will you still love me then?"

"Of course." She chuckled. She reached up and touched the side of his face, where laugh lines were sure to materialize in the years to come. "I'll love you no matter how wrinkly you get."

"Someday your hair is going to turn silver, and this dress might get too tight on you, and I'm still going to want you just as much as I do *right this minute.*" Ian raised his eyebrows suggestively and pulled gently at the silky fabric. *Right here, right now, would she be willing?* It was worth a try. "You know, maybe we shouldn't wait until the dress gets too tight. Maybe we should just take it off *now."*

"Right now?" Megan lifted one eyebrow and scooted closer on the sofa. "Are you suggesting we should lock that door?"

"I don't know…" Ian's heart raced. "I promised myself years ago that I'd never lock the door to my dressing room."

"Are you ready to break that promise to yourself?" Megan asked, biting her lower lip.

"More than you could possibly *imagine."* Ian's husky voice pierced through his whisper.

"I have a really creative imagination…" Megan whispered.

Ian didn't hesitate. He lifted himself off his knees and stepped over to the door. With one hand he turned the lock, with the other he flicked off the light, knowing it wouldn't be difficult to find that sofa in the dark.

CHAPTER SEVEN:
ON SOLID GROUND

"I need to talk to you, brotha'." Nathanial shuffled his feet nervously as he stood on Ian's doorstep. Nathanial had never come to Ian's home before, and he seemed uncomfortable.

"Come on in, mate." Ian stepped aside to welcome him into the house.

"Could we go for a walk?" Nathanial glanced over Ian's shoulder at Megan standing a few feet back in the hallway. It was clear that whatever Nathanial had to say, he wanted to say it to *just* Ian or he would have waited to talk to him at rehearsals later in the day. Ian looked back at his wife, shrugged, grabbed his light jacket and walked out into the morning air. They got a few steps away from the house and finally Nathanial took a deep breath. "I want to know where I stand."

"What are you talking about?" Ian questioned as they walked slowly down the long driveway.

"Something you said the other night at the awards show got me confused," he admitted. "You told the world that Gary was going to be taking a little *break* from the band."

"Yeah…" Ian hesitated. "How is that confusing?"

"Where does that leave me?" Nathanial asked. "Am I just here until Gary decides to come back? Am I just a placeholder until your *real* drummer gets cleaned up and sober and is able to function in society again? Is that all I am?"

Realization hit Ian, and he had to stop Nathanial. It wasn't easy. Stopping a man that big would have been easier if Ian were Ed's size, but he finally got Nathanial to turn and look at him.

"Am I just an extra?" Nathanial asked, kicking a stone in the driveway. "Just a pawn on the stage you're moving around to your liking?"

"Nathanial." Ian spoke plainly, clearly, with no teasing, no joking, and no hesitation. "*You* are Buxton Peak's drummer now. *Forever,* as far as I'm concerned."

Nathanial looked away from Ian, down to the pavement at his feet, back up, and finally met him eye to eye.

"Having Gary on that stage was a formality. It

was a last goodbye… and an introduction. It was a good transition, if you really think about it."

"I guess that makes me feel better." Nathanial spoke quietly, turned, and kept walking. "I'm sorry you and I got off on the wrong foot. I can be really headstrong sometimes, and I don't like being told what to do. Being the drummer is like always being in the background; you're *literally* at the back of the stage."

"Maybe we should put you up front and center." Ian teased. "We can put this huge set of drums up in the front, and I'll stand in the back with just my little microphone, since I'm a scrawny little dude."

"Never gonna let me live that one down, are you?" Nathanial laughed, and got serious again. "I didn't understand it before, but now after jamming with you for the past couple of months, seeing how you are with the guys at the youth program, and seeing how people respond to you at social gatherings, in the recording studio, and at that awards show, I see you differently. You're not just the cocky, little jerk I thought you were at first. You're a natural leader, with this weird magnetism that draws people to you. It's almost surreal."

Ian wasn't sure how to respond to that. He was reminded of the conversation between him and Jeremy when he'd been told the same thing.

He'd always known that people were drawn to him, but he was never really sure why. He had to admit that sometimes it did go to his head and made him a little cocky, but there was always someone or something that would knock him back off the little pedestal and remind him where he really stood, and that was in God's light. That's what drew people to him. He was shining the light of Christ through every part of him. Goofy kid, passionate husband, devoted son and brother, singer and songwriter, rock star, band member, community and church member, all of it was part of a whole that was only complete because of his love for God.

The realization brought him a sudden feeling of humility. He took a deep breath that ended with a sigh and a smile. He didn't need to respond. Nathanial understood it too. They walked along together, as brothers and friends, no need for words, just enjoying the beauty of another Nashville morning. The future felt right, and it was time to take the next steps, together.

* * * * * * * * *

"I'm not sure how we're going to do this." Ian closed the door to the recording studio behind him and pulled up a chair next to Kai. He turned to Andy, effectively including him in the conversation as well. "I need your input and suggestions. We need a new routine and a new ritual. We can't do things the way we've always done them."

Kai and Andy nodded their heads, but Nathanial just sat there waiting. He already knew this discussion was coming because of the conversation he and Ian had earlier in the day.

"Nathanial is not Gary, and he's nothing like Gary." Ian's gaze shifted toward the drum set. Nathanial held up a stick and twirled it in his right hand. Ian rolled his eyes. "Okay, maybe in some ways you're alike."

"I have a much nicer tan," Nathanial joked.

"The point is," Ian said. "We are not the same guys we were when we started this band."

"Yeah, you and Kai have transitioned to sleeping with girls instead of each other." Andy had such a stoic expression that Nathanial almost missed the joke. After a pause, Nathanial jerked his head around and gaped at Ian.

"You have to admit," Kai interjected. "Even after all these years, Ian is still really hot." He casually draped his arm around the back of Ian's chair.

"Is he..." Nathanial stammered. "Are you?"

"No, we're not!" Ian grabbed a guitar pick off the table and flicked it at Andy. "The guys used to tease me and Kai that we liked each other instead of girls."

"I still don't understand why they would think that." Kai raised his eyebrows, ran his thumb in circles on Ian's shoulder, and batted his eyelashes.

"Will you stop?" Ian tried to shrug out from under Kai's arm. He pushed Kai away, but couldn't hide the sparkle in his eyes. "I haven't slept with you in years."

"Wait, you've… slept together?"

"Every… single… night." Andy doubled over with laughter.

"Ian is very warm and snuggly." Kai nodded and somehow kept a completely straight face.

"Mates, he doesn't know you're joking," Ian said, standing up from his chair and walking over to the side table to pour himself a glass of water. Nathanial played along for a moment more.

"Brotha' I am an ordained minister," Nathanial said. "I've offered many parishioners counsel about how to handle their inherent desires toward…"

"This isn't the kind of advice I was looking for." Ian's cheeks turned red. "The point I was trying to make is we need to start some new traditions. What has always worked before is not what's going to work now."

"Yeah, Megan would not appreciate me sneaking into your hotel room." Kai folded his arms across his chest and leaned back in his chair. "You'll have to get along without me."

"I think I'll get on just fine, thank you." Ian downed a glass of water, turned toward the group, and rested his hands on the table behind him. "We need a new pre-show routine."

Nathanial had no idea what their regular routine *had* been. He'd never performed for a stadium full of people and had never rehearsed on a darkened stage in an eerily quiet stadium. He'd never stood in a green room with fans coming in for meet & greets, and photographs. He'd never been a part of something this big. So he wasn't prepared for Ian to look to him for advice.

"What did you and your band always do before your shows?" Ian inquired. It took Nathanial a few seconds to realize that Ian was talking to him. It took him a moment more for him to realize that he didn't remember a routine per se. After that, a bigger realization came into his heart.

"*My* band… is Buxton Peak." Nathanial stated firmly and with conviction. "We are still in the process of deciding what *we* do before our shows, because *we* have yet to perform live together. We're taking each day as it comes."

At that point, four heads were nodding. This was truly a process, and they were developing it little by little, together.

"Well, that's alright then." Ian pushed himself away from the table and paced the floor. "Next month is our first show, and it's right here in Nashville at the Bridgestone Arena, which is great because it's close to home."

Nathanial thought it was weird for Ian to refer to Nashville as "home" since they'd only been living here for seven months, yet it felt very *right*. This *was* home now, for the foreseeable future. Kai and Rhonda had bought a house together within a few blocks of Ian and Megan. Andy had moved in with Vanessa in an apartment close to Nathanial and Monique's modest home near the church. They were all very settled here. Yeah, this was home. He nodded in agreement.

"You know what would be cool?" Kai leaned forward and fiddled with the arm of his guitar, still resting in its stand. "We should all go down there before the crew sets up and help decide where everything will be displayed, and how it should be arranged and really get involved in the whole process."

"That's a great idea." Andy agreed. "I have no clue what happens beforehand. I've always showed up on the day of the show and the stage is magically just *there.*" He shrugged.

"What's it going to be like performing sober?" Kai teased him.

"I don't know." Andy laughed nervously. "I'll tell you afterward." They all smiled warmly at him, clearly proud that he'd been clean for almost a year now. It was quite an accomplishment.

"Well, I hope this doesn't make you even more nervous…" Ian stopped pacing and grinned at them. "But we've sold out the Bridgestone, so we're looking at around 18,000 people. Not our biggest show ever, but it's big."

"Speak for yourself," Nathanial said, fiddling with his drumsticks. "I've never performed for more than a couple hundred. This is going to be downright terrifying for me."

"All the more reason why it will be a good idea for us to be very involved in the planning and set up." Ian observed. "I'll tell Jeremy to talk with the production team and get us into the arena as soon as possible. This is going to be fun."

"How *do* you deal with a space that big, brotha'?" Nathanial asked. "I can't even imagine it. I mean, I've been to the arena once when I took the youth to an NCAA basketball tournament a few years back, but we were in the nose-bleeder seats. This is going to be completely different."

"Well, that does bring up one point I want to address." Ian got a little more serious. "I've had a little pre-show ritual that I'd really like to continue, if that's alright with the rest of you.

Nathanial, the other guys know all about it, but I should let you know. I'm a little bit… particular about certain things."

"You don't say…" Nathanial teased him sarcastically. That made all of them chuckle, and it lightened the mood. "Do go on, fearless leader…"

"As I was saying…" Ian smiled over at him. "I like to have the stadium or arena completely quiet for rehearsals. No distractions, no spectators, no workers moving things around, nothing. Just us and the instruments."

"Well…" Kai interrupted. "First *you* and the instruments, and then you allow us into your sacred space. Am I right?" Kai smiled over at Ian, just barely teasing.

"Okay, okay." Ian admitted. "I prefer to have a few minutes to myself. That's not to say it has to *stay* that way. It's just the way we've always had it. As I said, I'm a bit particular. But things are different now."

"Brotha'," Nathanial cut in. "If it works for you, we'll make it work for us. Okay?" Ian looked like he appreciated that Nathanial understood him. Nathanial had the same creative mind Ian had.

"Thank you." Ian nodded over to him and then tilted his head as if he just had a realization. "I don't *think* I'm going to sit at your drum set though, like I used to at Gary's."

"Why?" Nathanial wasn't sure if he was asking why Ian usually sat at Gary's drum set, or why he *didn't* want to sit at Nathanial's. He just left it open ended to see how Ian would respond."

"It's kind of like…" Ian thought for a second, rubbing his hand along his chin. "Like your drum set is *your* sacred space."

"Maybe you should get yourself your own set of drums." Kai suggested. "You've got a big enough house now." They all snickered and chuckled. Ian had purchased one of the larger estates in the greater Nashville area when deciding where to settle down. It was almost embarrassing how much space they had to themselves. The guys had all joked that Ian and Megan could have ten children and still have plenty of room. Not that they seemed to be in any hurry.

"I think I might just do that," Ian said. "What a great idea, mate."

"All right. We're starting to form a plan," Nathanial said, nodding. "The rest will work itself out. For now, let's get some practice time in. Taisha's going to be done with her playdate in a few hours, and I like to have dinner together as a family as often as we can."

"I look forward to that." Kai smiled at Nathanial. "My little guy is about to turn one in a few months. He's just starting to eat real food. Being a dad is the best thing ever."

"You got that right, brotha'." Nathanial nodded at Kai, turned to his drums, and passionately let loose on the set. He finally felt as if he was where he needed to be with his music, and he wasn't holding back.

Kai plugged in, started fast and hard, and he was joined by Andy's powerful bass. Ian didn't wait long to wail into the microphone with his strong vocals. They were finally more than just a group of guys practicing. They were Buxton Peak.

*   *   *   *   *   *   *   *   *

The first thing Nathanial noticed was the smell of new carpeting. He hadn't realized they'd finally gotten it installed. It was a welcome change from the fresh-paint smell that had been present for the past few months. As Nathanial proceeded down the hall at the back end of the church, he was plunged into darkness. He heard whispers coming from the youth center. *What are they up to?*

He decided to sneak up on the kids and came around the corner, flipping on the light, expecting to surprise them. *What the heck?* No one was in the youth center, but it looked beautiful. Elegant colors graced the walls, quality furnishings were placed in inviting arrangements, beckoning the kids to lounge and interact with one another. Study areas were set up, computer stations were available, and the kitchen had new appliances and countertops. And, yes, the Berber carpet was newly installed. It all came together.

Nathanial heard a noise from the gym and snickered. *They can't hide from me.* He crept down another darkened hallway toward the gym. This time when he opened the door, the light switch wouldn't work. Instead, a sparkling silver disco ball lit up, throwing twinkling lights spinning through the gym. A room full of people yelled at once.

"Surprise!"

Nathanial's drum set was prominently displayed at one end of the gym along with guitars in stands and microphones and speakers and amplifiers. It looked like a high-school dance with Buxton Peak as the live entertainment. The gym was filled with hundreds of people smiling, cheering, and clapping. Kids from the youth center smiled and came forward to pat Nathanial on the back, give him fist bumps, and slap high-fives. Parishioners from the church were there, kids of all ages, and the guys from the band. They were all there to celebrate with him.

This wasn't just a celebration of the renovated youth center; it was a celebration of Nathanial's new job and the start of his new life. He put his hand over his eyes and choked back sobs. It was all too much.

Little Taisha ran up and climbed into Nathanial's arms. He held her and bounced her, grinning through his tears. Monique came up and wrapped her arms around the two of them, whispering to him. "I'm so proud of you."

"I love you, Monique." Nathanial pulled away and looked down into her beautiful brown eyes. "Thank you for joining me on this journey."

"I wouldn't miss a minute of our lives together, and I'm so happy to be here today."

Reverberation from the microphone startled them, and Ian's voice came across the loudspeakers. "Can I have your attention, please?"

Everyone turned to where Ian stood with Kai and Andy near the bandstand, and a hush fell over the room. Nathanial shifted his daughter to one arm and wrapped his other around his wife.

"We're getting close to heading out on tour, and we thought you'd all like to be the first to hear the new-and-improved Buxton Peak, with Pastor Nathan as our new drummer." Ian held out his arm toward Nathanial, and the room erupted in applause.

Nathanial's throat tightened, and his heart warmed. This was such a stark contrast to his life a year ago, trying to pull nickels out of pennies and support these youth. Here he was leaving them to join a rock band, heading out on tour and making more money than he ever thought possible. But these were the people who had loved him all along and supported him these past few years as he'd served the youth. He felt God's love all around him in this gym full of people.

"It's just a couple of songs," Ian continued. "But I think you're going to like them."

"You got any rap songs in that set?" Scott called out.

"Would you like us to?" Ian questioned, laughing a little. The kids nodded and smiled back, knowing this hard rock band would likely not be able to rap. "We'll do something even better. We'll have an open-mic right after Buxton Peak performs. You guys come up and show us what *you've* got."

"Sweet." More fist bumps, more grins, more cheers.

"I've got one more surprise." Ian grinned. "The first concert on our tour is here at the Bridgestone Arena, and you're all getting free tickets!" The room erupted in applause and cheers again.

Nathanial kept Taisha in his arm and held Monique's hand as he made his way through the crowd to the other end of the gym where his band waited for him. It took a long time to meander through the room. Everyone wanted to shake his hand or clap him on the back. When he got to the little stage, Ian was the last person to shake his hand before he gestured for Nathanial to join them.

Nathanial set Taisha down and leaned over to kiss Monique. She giggled and winked at him.

"Go get 'em, tiger!" Monique whispered to just him.

"You be waiting for me right here, sugar."

"You know I will," Monique said.

Nathanial stepped away from his family to join his band on the stage. He sat down at the drum set and pulled a set of drumsticks from the pocket of his sport coat, where he always had a set available. *You never know when you might need a set of drumsticks.*

With a jerk of his chin toward Ian, Nathanial twirled the stick in his right hand and let loose on the drums. Kai joined with his screaming guitar, and Andy followed up on the bass. Ian added his powerful vocals, starting off their first song just as they'd practiced in the studio hundreds of times. This felt real and whole. Nathanial left it all on the stage that night and played with his whole heart and soul. *I'm home…*

CHAPTER EIGHT:
STUPID QUESTIONS

"The last time you took us to one of these temples, you *left* us for two years. That's not going to happen again, is it?" Kai asked.

Ian understood Kai's frustration. During Buxton Peak's second North American tour, the band had taken a detour to visit the historic temple in Kirtland, Ohio. While sitting in a pew alone, Ian had the distinct impression to set aside his music for two years and serve as a full-time missionary. The other guys in the band were furious.

"That was different," Ian said. "You can't actually go into this one." Ian nodded in the direction of the Nashville temple. They had to drive past the beautiful building on their way to pick up their tuxedos, and Ian asked Kai to pull into the parking lot and stop a moment.

"I didn't go in the other one, either." Kai said. Although the one in Kirtland was no longer owned by The Church of Jesus Christ of Latter-day Saints, or used in an official capacity, Ian had insisted the entourage take a detour so he could visit Ohio.

"But you *could* have." Ian pulled his thoughts back to the present and gazed at the comparably-smaller building in front of him. The Nashville temple was simple and elegant, but not as grand as some of the larger, more famous LDS temples.

"Why can't we go in this one?" Kai followed Ian's example and studied the building's exterior.

"I can," Ian said. "You can't."

"What makes you so special?" Kai asked. "Never mind, stupid question. Everything about you is special. Why are *you* allowed to go in, but not *me?*" Ian was accustomed to Kai's offhand compliments, so this one didn't faze him. It was still humbling.

"Because I've taken the preparation classes that are required," Ian said. "The things we learn in the temple are very sacred."

"You mean secret." Kai sneered.

"No, I mean *sacred*. You need to be prepared to learn the higher laws of the Gospel. But, you could get prepared… if you wanted."

"In time for Ed and India's wedding

tomorrow?" Kai raised his eyebrows.

"No, not that quickly." Ian shook his head.

"Well, enlighten me, preacher boy. What does it take to get prepared?"

"For starters, your body needs to be pure and clean, which means you'd have to give up alcohol." Ian bit his lower lip and took a sidelong glance at his best mate.

"Not happenin'." Kai shook his head and waved his hand dismissively. "Next."

"You can't be living with your girlfriend… or having sex outside of marriage at all."

"Ah, so we're back to the discussion on purity again." Kai pushed Ian's shoulder playfully. "You know darn well *that's* not happening. What else?"

"You'd have to be baptized and become a member of the Church… among other things, ya know, like a testimony that God *exists*."

"I'm an atheist. You know that."

"By choice," Ian mumbled.

"Yeah, so?"

"You could choose *not* to be an atheist," Ian said. Ian firmly believed the only way Kai was going to know God was real is if he chose to open his heart. After Kai's baby and girlfriend nearly died during childbirth, Ian felt the miracle of two priesthood blessings. He hoped Kai would have felt that as well. There had been plenty of opportunities for Kai to experience God's presence. Ian couldn't imagine looking down into a newborn baby's face and not see God's love lying right there in his arms.

"So anyway, it's a beautiful day in Nashville, and my best mate is about to go in and witness his bodyguard get hitched." Kai tried to change the subject to less-serious topics.

"Hitched?" Ian shook his head and chuckled. "They are going to be sealed for time and all eternity."

"Yeah, well I think it's *time* to go pick up our tuxedos and get ready for them to do this sealing thing."

"You know, he's way more than a bodyguard to me, right?" Ian whispered.

"I'm not jealous, Ian." Kai's defensive tone was not lost on Ian. "The two of you have this weird spiritual connection that I will never understand."

"And you and I have a weird musical connection that he will never understand." Ian felt a kinship with Kai that was deeper than any other relationship in his life, second only to Megan.

"You know, you're a really great brother to all of us." Kai finally turned his attention directly to Ian. "I never dreamed any of this could happen. When I first met you in music class back in primary school, and you knew how to play piano better than the teacher, I thought you were very strange."

"But you didn't look at me like I was strange." Ian leaned against the opposite door and hooked his leg up on the seat so he was facing Kai. "You had this wonderment in your eyes that I didn't understand. Everyone else looked at me like there was something wrong with me. But you looked at me like you were in awe of my talent."

"I was," Kai acknowledged. "I still am."

"Sometimes I feel so inadequate." Ian stared out the window. "Like if the world knew how stupid I really am, they wouldn't think I was so great."

"Well, let's not have them find out." Kai turned back to the steering wheel and put the car back in drive. "Because we need to keep you as the hottest rock star on the planet so we can pay for this Mercedes I just bought." Kai carefully backed out of his parking spot and tapped the accelerator.

"You drive like an old man." Ian huffed as Kai crept out of the parking lot at a turtle-pace. "This is an old man's car."

"At least I'm driving. When are you going to learn to drive?" Kai kept both hands on the wheel.

"I don't need to drive. I snap my fingers and people take me where I want to go."

"Very funny," Kai said.

"Like you, driving me around in your old man's car." Ian pursed his lips together, trying to keep up his haughty charade.

"The Mercedes Maybach is a fine, luxury sedan." Kai smoothed the steering wheel with his hands.

"I'll say it again. It's an old man's car."

"It's safe," Kai said. "I'm a dad now, remember? I gotta keep baby Sean wrapped in luxurious safety."

"Old man," Ian mumbled under his breath.

"I'll show you an old man." Kai floored the accelerator, proving that his new Maybach could go from zero to sixty in five seconds. He didn't let off the gas and they leapt forward as if the car wanted to fly off the road.

"Okay, okay, you've proven your point!" Ian cried out as his body was pressed against the seat from sheer force. "Now, slow down before you get us killed."

"Who's the old man, now?" Kai laughed, but let off the gas to bring the sedan to a more reasonable speed. They settled into a comfortable silence as they drove the last few miles to pick up the tuxedos.

* * * * * * * * *

"The temple wedding was beautiful," Megan said. Ian held her in his arms on the dance floor, gazing down into her eyes.

"Almost as beautiful as ours." Ian reached up and ran the backs of his fingers down her jawline. Her upswept curls interwoven with tiny white flowers were so different than the way she usually chose a straight simplicity. He loved her natural look, but tonight he couldn't take his eyes off his wife.

"Do you ever wish we'd had a reception like this?" Megan asked.

"No way!" Ian leaned closer to whisper in her ear. "That would have taken too long. I just wanted to get you to the hotel."

"Ian Taylor, you're a bad boy!" Megan smacked him lightly on his arm.

"You know what they say… behind every bad boy, there's a bad girl."

"I've never heard that before." Megan shook her head with a playful grin. She bit her lower lip and her eyes sparkled. Ian wanted to pull her off that dance floor and take her home. Instead he spun her around in a graceful dance and tried to keep his mind out of their bedroom and stay here in the ballroom.

The reception was simple and understated, but extravagant. It also included a host of entourage who hadn't been together in over a year.

All the other bodyguards for the band were in attendance, as were the producers, stage designers, tour managers, and even the bus drivers.

Everyone loved Ed and they were all happy to see him finally find true happiness with his beautiful and elegant supermodel giraffe, or so Ian called her during his toast. That drew endearing laughter and was the catalyst to an evening of dancing and partying.

Although the reception was intended to celebrate Ed and India's marriage, it turned into a great opportunity to get the whole crew to Nashville. They were ready to get back to work.

"I know you're the best man, and I'm the matron of honor, but… how much longer do we have to stay at the party?" Megan pulled at both of Ian's lapels and held him a few inches away from her face.

"Woman, are you a mind reader?" Ian's heart raced, staring into those seductive hazel eyes.

"I'm a body-language reader."

"I'll show you body language." Ian leaned in close and kissed Megan's neck a little more passionately than was acceptable in public.

"Patience, Mr. Taylor. We're supposed to be celebrating Ed and India's wedding right now."

"I'm quickly losing patience, Mrs. Taylor." Ian still hadn't pulled away, and his breath was very close to Megan's ear. "Let's go home and celebrate by ourselves."

"Do we have to?" Megan's pouty lips and batting eyelashes confused Ian. "I mean, we are standing in the ballroom on the main floor of one of Nashville's most luxurious hotels."

Ian felt a growl in the back of his throat as the reality of her statement played into his mind. Without even saying goodbye to their friends, Ian swept his wife off the dance floor and into the lobby. He had the credit card out of his wallet faster than he realized possible and slapped it onto the counter.

His eyes never left Megan's while Ian spoke to the desk clerk. "Could my wife and I get a hotel room... please?"

CHAPTER NINE:
GOODBYE AND HELLO

"We need to talk." Jeremy hesitated. "I'm glad you're all here... and that you haven't already heard it from someone else."

"What is this elusive thing that we've supposedly not heard?" Ian teased him, looking up from the guitar he was holding. Jeremy's pained expression immediately alerted Ian that something was very wrong. He stood up and walked over to his manager. "What is it, mate?"

"There's been an accident." Jeremy looked over at Kai and then Andy. He glanced briefly at Nathanial and looked back at Ian. "I don't even know how to say this..."

"Come here, mate." Ian guided Jeremy over to a chair in a rare display of role reversal. "It's alright, it's gonna be alright."

"No, Ian," Jeremy looked up at him. "It's not. Gary was in a very bad car accident last night. He wrapped his car around a tree going about 110 miles an hour."

"What hospital is he in?" Ian jumped up from his chair and reached for his jacket, as if he was ready to go to the airport and fly to London immediately.

"Ian…" Jeremy reached up and grabbed his arm. "There wasn't much left of him at the scene. He's gone, Ian."

"No," Ian whispered. He shook his head as his voice grew progressively louder. "That's not possible. He was just here, two weeks ago for the awards show. He was very stoned… as he always is… what was he doing behind the wheel of a car? Who gave him permission to drive a vehicle? He should *never* drive. He's never *sober* enough to drive. Where was his driver? Who was supposed to be taking care of him?" Ian crumpled to the floor on his knees, hands gripping his hair as if pulling it would somehow lessen the pain in his heart.

Kai sat down hard on a chair and stared off into the corner. Andy dropped to his knees and sobbed. Nathanial just sat at his drums and bowed his head, praying silently. Jeremy sat next to Ian and rubbed his shoulder, trying to comfort his young friend.

This was a moment in life that none of them would ever forget.

*   *   *   *   *   *   *   *   *

Ian walked quietly forward to where Gary's mother sat alone at the front of the little chapel. Most of the mourners wouldn't be arriving for another few hours, but Ian wanted a few minutes by themselves. He came and sat at Helen's feet and wrapped his arms around her. It was the first time in several days that he gave himself permission to completely let go and allow the grief to crush him. He felt safe in her arms.

This was a woman who had packed lunches for the guys when they wanted to hike up into the hills and stocked her refrigerator with enough junk food to keep teenage boys' hunger at bay. She let the guys take over her basement with drum sets and guitars and microphones and enormous speakers and amplifiers. She put up with them back when they sounded terrible, and she always encouraged them. It was never a question for her *if* her boys would become rock stars; it was always *when*. She had complete faith in them. Now she was without all of her boys. Ian, Kai, and Andy were in America... with a new drummer. And her Gary was about to be laid to rest forever.

"I never thought to hide his car keys," Helen whispered. Her fingers brushed through Ian's hair as he laid his head in her lap. His sobs had lessened to a rhythmic sniffle every few seconds. He felt as if he may break again at any moment so he held very still and let his surrogate mother hold him as if she were holding Gary. Ian wished she were. "He came and went so frequently. He'd come home and sleep for a few days, sober up a little, and disappear again. I thought rehab would help. He needed to go back in. I knew that. I tried to talk him into it, but he would get mad at me and leave again. Eventually I stopped trying. I was just so thankful that he was home and safe for those few days that I didn't bother him while he was home. I should have forced him to go back."

"He was an adult." Ian sat up so he could face her. "You can't force an adult into rehab. All you can do is try. You can't blame yourself for not trying hard enough."

"All those times he came and went, I always knew there was the possibility that one day… he wouldn't come back." She put one hand on each side of Ian's face, as if he was a little boy. "That 'one day' has come, hasn't it?"

"Yeah," Ian whispered. "It has." Helen lowered herself off her chair so that she was sitting on the floor next to Ian, and they held each other and cried. They didn't speak again. They didn't need to. There was an unspoken understanding of love and grief for Gary.

∗　∗　∗　∗　∗　∗　∗　∗　∗

The basement door was closed, and Ian just stared at it. Everyone else was in the living room, eating the obligatory after-funeral luncheon, but he had quietly snuck away. He knew what was on the other side of that door, and he knew what was at the bottom of those stairs. Did he really want to take that journey? He knew exactly what would happen if he did.

He lingered in the kitchen for several minutes before walking carefully forward. The creak of the door was barely audible, but he turned his head to see if anyone had heard and would come around the corner to scold him for invading his friend's private space. No one came to check, and he quickly tucked himself into the dark stairwell and pulled the door shut behind him.

He didn't even bother turning on the light until he reached the bottom of the stairs, where he knew he'd find the switch that turned on the colored, sparkling disco ball, which hung from the ceiling. Flicking on that switch was like stepping back in time to when they were teenagers, not so long ago. Before they were more than potential, before his mission service, before they were famous, before marriage and children and break-ups and drug abuse and crashed cars. Back when life was defined by simple, spinning, colorful lights.

The lights reflected the shine on the cymbals and the silver rim of the snares. A few guitars and bass guitars hung on stands, forgotten and out of tune. A few microphones were even plugged into speakers. Nothing was covered in dust. Gary must have been here recently, or his mom regularly kept it all cleaned as if ready for her boys to return. They never would.

As if in a dream, Ian stepped forward and gingerly sat at the drum set. A set of sticks waited at the ready. Did he dare? How loud would it be from upstairs? He couldn't hear them talking and eating and walking around. Would they be able to hear him? He picked up the sticks and just held them, caressing the wood gently. He closed his eyes and visualized Gary sitting here. What would his expression show? Peace, resignation, preparedness, readiness, eager to get started.

Without realizing he was even doing it, Ian spun the stick in his right hand and began to play as if he played every day. He didn't think about the noise or who might hear him or what they might think. He just played with heart and soul and life. His breathing was even and steady, his eyes half closed, in a zone that usually only existed on stage or in a recording studio. This was Gary's original stage and his original recording studio. This was his original rehearsal room. This was home.

Ian didn't hear them come down the stairs, and he didn't know they were in the room until suddenly there they were, strapping guitars around their shoulders and reaching for picks and turning knobs on amplifiers and speakers. He never stopped playing as Kai & Andy tuned their instruments, worked a few scales, and suddenly they were all playing together in a rhythm that was uniquely theirs.

This was Buxton Peak. Not Buxton Peak with a new drummer or a missing drummer or a missing anything. This *was* Buxton Peak, playing as if Gary was right there with them. The hurt and anger was forgotten. The fighting and drugs and betrayal were gone. The brotherhood was here. Not that it was *back*, it was just *here*.

They played for a very long time. It could have been hours. They jammed to several classic Buxton Peak songs, *Cavendish Fire*, *Stone Ridge*, *Manchester Heights*. They never slowed the rhythm down enough to play *Passing Through Eternity*, almost as if on purpose. They fell back into their original inspirations, *You Give Love a Bad Name* by Bon Jovi, *Angel* by Aerosmith, *Paradise City* and

Sweet Child of Mine by Guns N' Roses. They avoided the Guns N' Roses song that launched Buxton Peak, *Welcome to the Jungle.* The drum solo would have thrown all of them over the edge. They needed closure, not tears. They needed to go back to their roots, but not quite that far.

Then, they just stopped and looked at one another and collectively took a deep breath before their usual group hug. When their arms came around each other's necks and their heads came together in the center, it felt whole. It felt right. They could do this. They could go forward now. They felt closure.

Ian's stomach growled, and he chuckled.

"How long's it been since you've eaten, pal?" Kai whispered. It was a rhetorical question. They'd been together for the better part of the past four days, and Ian had yet to eat anything. Ian had pushed food away anytime someone tried to hand it to him, since the day they'd heard the news.

"Let's go upstairs." Ian's legs felt heavy and weak as he trudged up the stairs. He went straight for the refrigerator and started digging. The house was quiet, and he wasn't even sure if there was anyone else still here. The guys had barely started pulling out leftovers when Helen and Megan came quietly into the kitchen.

Ian took a step towards Megan and pulled his

wife into his arms. He didn't cry or speak or communicate anything other than the peace of having her with him. He just held her, knowing he'd neglected to let her in since the time he'd learned of Gary's death. He'd talk to her later. For now he just wanted to hold her. His stomach growled again.

"Okay, okay." Ian relented, chuckling. He looked down into Megan's eyes and smiled playfully. "Get me some food woman."

"It's about time." Megan looked over at Kai and winked at him, obviously thankful that whatever they'd done in the basement had brought back her husband.

"Where are the others?" Andy inquired.

"Vanessa and Rhonda took that adorable baby back to the hotel so he could sleep," Helen told them. "We didn't want to interrupt the concert, but they needed some rest. Congratulations, by the way." She was still looking directly at Andy, but he shook his head quizzically.

"About what, Mrs. Owens?"

"Please, Andy." She looked hurt. "After all these years, you *know* to call me Mum."

"Sorry, Mum." Andy grabbed a roll off the counter and took a large bite without even putting butter on it.

"Congratulations about your baby." Helen told Andy.

"Oh, that's not my baby." Andy explained with a full mouth. "That's Kai's baby."

"No, no." She shook her head. "Vanessa's *your* girlfriend, isn't she?" All conversation in the room stopped, and Andy stopped chewing and just stared at Helen.

"Vanessa's… not pregnant." Andy gulped.

"Of course she is." Helen guffawed. "Can't you tell?"

Andy shook his head and looked over at the other guys in shock; they all stared back at him with confusion.

"Megan?" Andy questioned. "Did you know?"

"I don't think *she* knows," Megan whispered. "If she did, we wouldn't have heard the end of it for the past few days or weeks. She's wanted a baby so bad I'm surprised she hasn't begged you for one by now. She must *not* know." They all turned to Helen.

"How is it that *you* know?" Andy asked.

Helen just laughed at them.

"It's *so* obvious. Can't you see the glow on her face?" Helen just shook her head and started helping make sandwiches for her hungry musicians, chuckling as she went. Conversation continued to cease, but eating resumed as they all stared ahead or looked at one another. Andy sat, chewing slowly and looking a little shocked.

Kai broke the silence.

"Mate…" Kai grinned at him. "Being a dad is the *best.*"

"I'll expect lots of brotherly advice on that." Andy looked terrified.

Megan cuddled next to Ian and put her arms around his waist. He looked down at her, she looked up at him, and they sighed together.

"Someday," Ian whispered.

"When God's ready," Megan said.

* * * * * * * * *

"Vanessa." Andy hesitated in the doorway of their hotel suite. "Are you doing okay?"

"I'm sleeping," she whispered. "What do you need?" She sat up halfway, trying to see him in the dark.

"Are you… feeling okay?"

"Why wouldn't I be?" She was a bit more awake and sounded confused. He came over beside her and knelt down next to the bed. He pulled her closer to him very carefully as if she were delicate and fragile. "Andy? Are *you* alright? What's going on?" Andy didn't answer her, but he pulled the covers back slightly and put his hand gently on her non-existent belly.

"Is it true?" He looked up at her lovingly. "Are you… gonna have my baby?"

"What?" Vanessa sat up all the way and looked

at him in shock. "I'm not pregnant. Do I look fat to you? Oh my gosh... do I?" She pushed him away and got up from the bed. She turned on the light switch and looked into the full-length mirror near the bathroom. She turned every which way to see if she looked like she'd gained any weight.

"No, you don't look fat. You look beautiful. It's just that... well Gary's mum thinks you're pregnant."

"Why would she think that?" Vanessa seemed confused.

"I don't know." He shrugged. "She said she could tell. She said it was really obvious. Megan said that you might not even know you were pregnant because otherwise you'd be talking about it non-stop. Is that true? Do you *want* a baby? We can have a baby if you want one. You should have said something. I don't think I'd mind being a dad. I mean, Kai & Nathanial seem to like being dads. I might."

"I'd love a baby." Vanessa smiled. "But... I don't think I'm pregnant."

"How would you know?" Andy asked naively. "Don't you have to take a test or something?"

"Well, yeah. If I *thought* I was pregnant, I'd take a test."

"Maybe you should."

"Maybe you're right." She shrugged and turned back to the mirror, scanning for any outward signs. She looked completely normal. But still, Andy stepped closer to her, smiled and put his hand on her belly again. "Let's not get our hopes up until we know one way or another."

But they grinned at each other, suspecting that they would soon be celebrating.

CHAPTER TEN:
WHEN GOD'S READY

"So, I learned some things from your mum while we were visiting after the funeral." Megan's grin told Ian that he was about to be hit by one of those embarrassing stories that only a mother can tell. He growled just slightly, pursing his lips playfully. He took a deep breath and closed his eyes.

"I'm afraid to ask." Ian opened one eye and cringed away from her.

"It's not that bad. What could you possibly have done in your life that makes you nervous like this?" Ian bent to pick up a small rock and threw it up the hill, toward Solomon's Temple. The ancient tower loomed just far enough away that the rock didn't even come close. He reached back and grabbed Megan's hand, pulling her farther toward the destination structure and bit his lower lip.

"I was not a very good little boy."

"Well, this story involves you as a man. As far as I'm concerned, you are a *very* good man." He pulled her close and held her in his arms, looking down into her flirting eyes.

"I'm liking this story a little better…"

"I heard all about your mission… and how you came to know Ed."

"Oh no, not this story." Ian leaned his head back and laughed. He unwrapped himself from his wife and pulled her by the hand, continuing up the hill. "You cannot believe a word that woman says."

"Now I *know* she's telling the truth, or you wouldn't be so embarrassed."

"Lay it on me," he said. "What did she tell you?"

"She said they almost had to pull you from the mission field."

"That was *not* my fault."

"She said they were about to put you into the Mission home as an Assistant to the Mission President." Megan stopped him again and he tried to hide his smile, knowing what was coming next. He looked off into the clear, blue sky, waiting for the inevitable punch line. "Until they realized you were packing the seats in the chapel."

"Packing the seats, huh?" Ian shuffled his feet and felt heat rush to his cheeks. "Is that the way she described it?"

"She said you were baptizing girls left and right."

Ian reached into his hair and gripped his perfectly random spikes of hair gel. "That's not true. Pure lies."

"Yeah right," Megan said. "Flirt to convert?"

"That's not what I was doing, I promise." He couldn't hide his guilty smirk, but looked down at her playful expression. "They just followed me everywhere. That's all."

"So the Mission President found the biggest, most intimidating missionary in the area and stuck you together as companions." She looked up at him with a knowing grin. "The Church provided you with a bodyguard."

"The Church did nothing of the sort." Ian leaned his head back and laughed. "Ed and I just became fast mates, that's all. We had a lot in common."

"You have nothing in common."

"My mum's telling you stories, that's all." They were almost to the top of Grinn's Hill, and he could see forever in all directions. "Just stories."

"She said you had to sit in the very back corner, with Ed between you and all the girls."

"Eh," Ian said. "I didn't notice any girls."

"She also said that they kept you and Ed together for the whole rest of your mission, even though normally companions get separated after a few months."

"Lies. All lies." Ian shook his head but couldn't hide his smile. "I'm ashamed that you'd believe your mother-in-law over your own husband."

"She tells me fun stories about my husband." Megan pulled herself closer to him, wrapping her arms around his waist and looking up into his eyes. He sighed as he gazed down at her. The flirtatious grin left her countenance, and a resolute smile pulled at the corners of her mouth. When he finally spoke, his voice was barely a whisper on the wind.

"Sorry I've been a little distant the past few days."

"It was understandable," Megan whispered back. "You and Gary used to be so close."

"I wish we could have left on better terms." Ian released her gaze and looked out across the peak. "I should have reached out to him more. He probably felt like we just replaced him. You know?"

"You sort of did, honey." Megan's accusing words caused Ian to look back down at her, hurt clouding his thoughts. "You couldn't go back to the way you were. What he did was wrong. I'm not sure Kai would have ever been able to work with Gary again. The drugs he gave Rhonda almost killed her and the baby. Plus, he needed help with his addictions. That wasn't something you could just fix."

"I don't know what I could have done differently," Ian said. "I wish I could go back in time and force him to quit drinking and doing drugs way back when he first started." Ian sat down hard, right there in the middle of the trail, and put his head between his knees.

"Well, you can't." Megan lowered herself beside him and wrapped her arm around his shoulders. "And, you can't blame yourself. He made his own choices. You weren't in charge of taking care of him, or his car keys."

"It still hurts…"

"I know it does, babe." Megan kept her arms around Ian while he sobbed for his lost friend.

It still hurts.

*   *   *   *   *   *   *   *   *

"Earth to Tyrell…" Nathanial had stolen the ball right out of his hands, moved around, and made an easy layup without Tyrell even noticing. He was staring off into the far corner as if he had seen a ghost. Nathanial's heart sped up. "Son, are you okay?"

"Huh?" Tyrell pulled his focus back, but that haunted look was still in his eyes. There was something else besides fear... guilt, maybe?

"What's the matter?" Nathanial turned all the way around so he was privy to Tyrell's obvious distraction. Mary sat at the corner table with Megan Taylor, who had her arm around the girl's shoulders. "Is Mary crying?"

"Maybe..." Tyrell mumbled. His eyes shifted away, and the fear was pushed away by the guilt.

"*What* did you do?" Nathanial put the ball on the gym floor and stepped on it, holding the ball in place. He folded his arms across his chest. Tyrell put both hands in his jeans pockets and continued to avoid eye contact. "You know why Mary's crying... don't you?"

"Maybe..." Tyrell looked Nathanial in the eye, scrunched up his shoulders, and quickly looked away again.

"Don't make me go talk to your mamma, boy. You tell me the problem."

"Probably gonna need to arrange that meeting anyway, Pastor Nathan." Tyrell shuffled his feet, and his shoulders slouched.

"So, we're talking about a really *big* problem."

Tyrell didn't speak again, just nodded once.

"How old are you now? Seventeen?" Nathanial waited for the nod in answer to his rhetorical question. "You excited about that college scholarship offer you been carrying around in your backpack? So... you just gonna go mess up your life before it even starts?"

Tyrell pulled himself to his full height, looking Nathanial in the eye, man-to-man, but a single tear ran down his cheek, and his lip quivered. A soft whisper escaped the young man's mouth. "I didn't mean to..."

"You didn't mean to what? Mess up your life? Or make a *really* poor decision?"

"I think... it was a series of poor decisions... that led to one big, huge, massive poor decision... that led to a whole lot'a bad decisions after that one."

"Yeah... I'll bet it did." Nathanial took a deep breath. *God, give me the patience I need in order to counsel this young man.* "Whatchu gonna do, son?"

"I dunno..." Tyrell gulped.

"You ready to be a father?"

"No sir, Pastor Nathan, I am not." Tyrell's voice wavered.

"Too late, though, ain't it?"

"Yes, sir..."

"You know who you remind me of?" Nathanial put his hand on Tyrell's arm. The young man's shoulders relaxed, and he let out his breath. "You remind me of myself."

"You?" Tyrell's eyebrows shot up. "...and

Sister Jackson?"

"Oh, heaven's no! We remained pure until our weddin' night!" Nathanial shoved Tyrell's arm gently and pulled him back around so they were looking each other in the eyes again. "You and lil' Mary look at each other the same way Sister Jackson and I look at each other about an hour before Taisha's bedtime. And you ain't lettin' her back outta your arms again, are you?"

"I sure don't want to, Pastor Nathan." Tyrell took a deep breath and let it out real slow.

"You got a place to live once you're married?" Nathanial asked.

"Married?" Tyrell's eyes were big and round.

"Y'all gonna be acting like a married couple, you better *be* a married couple."

Tyrell gulped, but nodded infinitesimally. "Yes sir, Pastor Nathan."

"Where are you living now?"

"My mamma's."

"What about Mary?"

"She stayin' at her sister's crib…"

"Yeah, I think she's been stayin' a few times at yours, too, ain't she?"

"Yes, sir…"

"Your mamma know that?"

"No, sir, she works third shift at the hospital."

"Yeah, I bet that breaks your heart, doesn't it?"

"Pastor Nathan, you know I never intended for any of this to happen." Tyrell pleaded with his eyes. "I love the Lord, I really do. I just, had a little bit of a tough time with one of His rules." He gulped again and remorse shone through his countenance.

"There's one more person besides the Lord from whom you're going to need to ask forgiveness, and that's your future wife." Nathanial looked pointedly into Tyrell's face. "Are you ready for this, son?"

"Not even a little bit, Pastor Nathan." Tyrell stood straight and raised his chin. "But, let's go." Tyrell gently pushed Nathanial out of the way and strode confidently in the direction of the far corner, where Mary still sat with Megan. Both women looked up when the men approached.

Tyrell didn't hesitate, but dropped to both knees in front of Mary and pulled her into his arms. He was tall enough that even on his knees he was able to look her in the eye from where she sat. Mary reached up and pushed a curl off Tyrell's forehead.

"Will you please forgive me for my indiscretions?" Tyrell let his question hang in the air as her shock turned to confusion. Her eyebrows creased, and her lip quivered.

"What did you do?" Mary asked.

"We," Tyrell corrected her. "It was what *we*

did… together. We didn't obey God's most precious law. He's going to forgive us. I know because He sent His Son as our Savior. Now, I need to know if you'll forgive me…"

Nathanial reached down and put his hand on Tyrell's shoulder. *Thank you Father for teaching this, thy son, your ways. Help him to become the man You want him to be. Help him to turn his life around.*

"Of course I forgive you, Tyrell," Mary whispered. "I love you."

"I love you, too, and that's why I want you to do two things for me." Tyrell put both his large hands on either side of her little face and brushed the tears from her cheeks.

"I'd do anything for you, Tyrell."

"First, I want you to marry me…" He took a deep breath and whispered, "…please."

"But, what about your college scholarship?" Mary's shoulders fell. "I don't want you to give up your dreams for me and…" Mary looked up at Nathanial and then over at Megan. Nathanial stepped over and placed both hands on Tyrell's shoulders, promising solidarity and counsel.

"And… our baby?" Tyrell nodded. Mary gulped and lowered her gaze, remorse pulling her shoulders down. She fidgeted with the hem of her shirt, and Tyrell lowered his hands to pick up both of hers, with the same tenderness that he'd held her face. "That's the other thing I want to talk to you about."

Mary looked up and a tear ran down each of her cheeks, but she held his gaze.

"We can live in married housing. You want to go to the University of Tennessee also, right?" Tyrell nodded. "But I don't think we're ready to be parents."

"I would never!" Mary pulled her hands away from his and clasped them across her stomach.

"No, sugar, I would never ask that of you!" Tyrell pulled her closer into his arms. "I just think we should find a couple who would be willing to adopt and care for our baby as their own."

"Then we would know our baby was loved and cared for," Mary whispered, looking up at Tyrell with hope in her eyes for the first time all day.

"When God's ready to bring a child into this world, he finds a way," Tyrell said.

Megan gasped. She'd been silent this whole conversation, sitting there with her arm around Mary's back. She pulled her hand away and clasped it to her heart. "...when God's ready."

Megan stood up and began pacing back and forth in a path near the wall. A panic overtook her countenance, and she started mumbling to herself.

"Megan, are you alright?" Nathanial stepped

over and put his hand on her arm. She didn't even glance at him.

"Ian and I have been saying that since we got married," Megan whispered. "When God's ready."

"But you don't have any children," Nathanial said, shaking his head.

"Not yet..." Megan's eyes filled with hope, and she rushed back over to where Mary and Tyrell sat holding each other's hands. Megan sat beside them and placed her hand on top of theirs, clasped in Mary's lap. "I think... if you'll allow us the honor... that Brother Taylor and I are meant to adopt your baby." Tears ran down Megan's cheeks. Happy tears, full of life and hope.

"Oh, Sister Megan! Would you?" Mary's face lit up with hope. The two women held each other's gaze, one a scared seventeen year old girl with her life ahead of her, and the other a young wife who had yet to conceive with her husband. It was as if Jesus was shining his light down upon the two of them, filling the room with a soft glow. The warmth in Nathanial's heart was unmistakable.

"God knows how to turn a difficult challenge into a beautiful blessing," Nathanial whispered. *Thank you, Jesus.*

* * * * * * * * *

"Ian!" Megan called from the front entryway. Ian heard the front door slam, and hard steps hurried through the hall and pounded down the basement stairs. She rushed around the corner, and her eyes scanned the small recording studio Ian had built. "Are you alone?"

"Yeah, babe." Ian set aside his Martin acoustic guitar and opened his arms. Megan sat in his lap and wrapped her arms around his neck. "What's up? You look excited."

"Ian, God's ready!"

"What? Are you finally pregnant?" Ian let go of her waist and reached one hand to her belly. Megan's smile fell, and her shoulders slouched. He was afraid she was going to tell him the news he'd suspected for a long time, that something was wrong and they weren't going to be able to have babies. He wanted to reassure her he loved her no matter what, so he smiled at her and tucked a loose strand of hair behind her ear.

"No… not yet." Her face scrunched into a grimace. "But Mary is!" Megan lifted herself back into a confident excitement.

"Who's Mary?" *I'm so confused.*

"Mary… you know, from the Youth Center!"

"Little Mary?" Ian lifted his eyebrows.

"She's seventeen," Megan said. "…and she's

not gonna be little for long."

"Oh my gosh… does the father know?"

"Oh, yes, it's Tyrell! And they're getting married!"

"Well, at least that's positive." Ian took a deep breath. "They're a little young to be parents. Didn't he *just* get a full-ride scholarship to play basketball for Tennessee?"

"Yes, and she's planning to go there, too. They'll live in married housing."

"Why are *you* so excited about all this?" Ian scratched his head.

"Because they've asked us to adopt their baby!"

Ian pushed Megan off his lap and leapt to his feet. Panic filled his stomach with fear. He held her arm for support.

"Wh-what? Like, forever?" His mouth went dry, and he reached for a water bottle, twisting the cap and squeezing at the same time. Water poured through the opening and dripped onto the floor. He reached for a towel and mechanically crouched down to wipe up his mess. *Adopt? A baby? … A baby.*

He stood quickly, spilling more water, but ignoring it this time. He dropped the towel on top of the mess and a powerful peace came over Ian as he looked down into the face of the most beautiful woman he'd ever seen. He somehow knew this was why they had yet to conceive. It wasn't meant to be. They were meant to be here in *this* place at *this* time to adopt *this* baby who needed a home.

"I'm gonna be a daddy?"

"Yeah," Megan said. The stressed panic on her face lessened to hope again. "If you want, I mean, we don't have to, if you don't want to."

"I'm gonna be a daddy," Ian whispered. Then he called out as if in a thankful prayer to Heavenly Father. "I'm going to be a daddy!" Ian picked Megan right off the floor and spun her around in his arms. He set her back on the floor and gazed into her beautiful hazel eyes, which were brimming with tears.

"I'm going to be a mum," Megan whispered.

"You're going to be an *amazing* mum," Ian whispered back before crushing his lips to hers in an embrace befitting a celebration. Their embrace and their kiss sealed the commitment. *If God's ready… I'm ready.*

CHAPTER ELEVEN:
BEFORE I LEAVE YOU

"I want to talk to both of you." Nathanial sounded like a stern father. Kai walked along beside him, wondering what was up. Nathanial didn't normally pull Kai and Andy aside like this. If he ever went for a walk with anyone, it was with Ian.

But today, Nathanial specifically requested some time alone with the other guys, and Ian stayed back at the studio. Ian seemed happy to have a little time alone with the instruments and his thoughts. He said he had ideas for some new songs and wanted to explore the sounds a little without an audience.

"You need to get married," Nathanial said. "I don't like this living together with your baby mammas."

"Our *what?*" Kai was startled by Nathanial's suggestion. He pulled Nathanial to a halt right in the middle of the sidewalk. Nathanial looked down his nose at Kai and narrowed his eyes.

"You had a child with your woman and never gave her, or him, your name. That's not right."

"That's none of your business," Kai said. But Nathanial wasn't done. He turned to Andy.

"And now you're gonna have a baby with your girlfriend, and it's not fair to her, or the baby, to not have a legal daddy."

"Our baby will have a daddy," Andy said. "I'll be its daddy." He pushed his long bangs out of his eyes, letting his hair blow in the soft breeze.

"I don't know how things are in England," Nathanial said, raising his eyebrows. "But in America, when a baby is born, the mamma's last name is on that baby's bassinette. And if the mamma don't have the same name as the daddy, then that baby don't have your name. And furthermore, it ain't right in God's eyes. You shouldn't even be livin' together or sleepin' together if you can't make it right with God."

"I don't believe in God," Kai scoffed. He shook his head dismissively. "There's no such thing as some supreme being who looks down on us in judgment."

"I'm sure that's what the fish in a tank think too, yet they're always willing to eat the food that floats down to them."

"That's an absurd comparison." Kai snorted, but didn't say anything more.

"I believe in God." Andy admitted. "And you're probably right. I need to marry Vanessa. Right away." He looked down at his feet.

"Well, I'm not marrying my girlfriend just because you give us some weird guilt trip." Kai narrowed his eyes. "*If* I marry her... ever... it will be because she and I *want* to get married, not because of some God who's going to smite us with a rod if we don't. That's ridiculous."

"Have you ever *asked* her if she wants to get married?" Nathanial challenged him.

"Why would I do that?" Kai demanded.

"Because every little girl dreams of their wedding day," Nathanial said. "They start picking out white dresses when they're six. They play Barbies, dress them all up in fancy dresses, and pretend that Ken walks them down the aisle, and they make them kiss. It's adorable. If you ever have a chance to watch little girls play, you'll see it. Women are just little girls who are taller and more cynical. Your woman wants to get married even if she won't admit it. Now if you care about her at all, or if you even care about your little boy, you need to give her that gift."

"Of course I love my little boy." Kai turned his nose up and looked away, not wanting to hear the truth.

"What about Rhonda?" Nathanial turned him back around and looked him right in the eye. "Do you love *her?*"

"Yeah…" Kai hesitated.

"Why do you sound so unsure?" Nathanial challenged. Kai didn't know how to answer that. It was true that he took her for granted, maybe even took advantage that she'd just be there even if he wasn't as committed as he should be. He even had to admit to himself that he sometimes got caught up in the attention he received from other women. He was a famous rock star. Women threw themselves at him. They always had. He had never cheated on Rhonda, but maybe the fact that they weren't married made it just a little easier to justify flirting with other girls a little bit more than he should. He suddenly felt confused and angry at Nathanial, as if he was insinuating something that wasn't far from the truth.

"I need some time to think." Kai pushed away from Nathanial's insistent hand on his shoulder and walked off, wishing this conversation had never happened.

*   *   *   *   *   *   *   *   *

"Can we talk?"

Rhonda was curled up on the couch with a novel in the quiet living room, waiting for little Sean to wake up from his nap. She looked up as Kai sat next to her with a very serious look on his face.

"What's wrong?" She set her book aside and creased her eyebrows.

"Nathanial just told me something that really messed with my head." He looked down at his hands and rubbed them on his knees. She reached over and stopped one of them, forcing him to look up at her. "He said I should marry you." She sank into the couch and shook her head slightly.

"I don't want you to marry me because some friend of yours talked you into it." She bristled. "If you want to marry me, it should be because *you* want to marry me."

"I kinda do." He looked at her sheepishly.

"You *kind of* do?" Rhonda almost choked. "That's not good enough either, Kai."

"I know." He agreed. "It's just that... I never really thought about it."

Rhonda didn't like that answer either. She shook her head in disgust and almost got up to walk away. But she suspected that this conversation was going to change their relationship in one direction or another and felt it best to hear him out.

"Nathanial told me that every little girl wants to get married and that I'm denying you that opportunity."

"In case you haven't noticed, Kai." Rhonda sneered at him. "I am *not* a little girl."

"I'm very aware of that, Rhonda." Kai looked up at her sheepishly. "I'm reminded of that every time I look into your beautiful eyes, and every time I hold your incredible body in my arms."

That softened her up a little, and she relaxed her shoulders. She even half-smiled at him. But she still looked away, and still felt hurt that in all this time that they'd been together, he had never once considered marrying her.

"He also told me that girls never really grow up; they just get more cynical, and I think that my denying you the opportunity to be married has made you a little jaded." Rhonda was kind of getting tired of what Nathanial thought about things but *was* interested to hear what Kai thought about it.

"Jaded, huh?" She considered that.

"I almost hauled off and decked Nathanial." Kai sighed. "But I went for a long walk and got to thinking about you and me and the future, and I honestly don't want to *ever* be with anyone else but you... ever."

"I feel the same way about you, Kai."

"So, that got me thinkin', that when we leave on tour next week…" He looked away for a second and took a deep breath before turning back and looking her right in the eye. "It wouldn't be a bad idea for me to have a ring on my hand when I left here."

Rhonda couldn't help smiling. He wasn't talking about planning a wedding for a year from now; he was talking about getting married now, this week, before he left on tour. She was reminded of the flicker of spark that had occurred between him and that young songstress at the awards show and knew that she would be very relieved to have a ring on his finger.

"Maybe tomorrow you and I could take a little trip to the jeweler down the street." He suggested.

"Sean will be up from his nap in a little while. We could go today. He might enjoy helping mommy pick out something pretty."

"As long as you don't let him hold it." Kai laughed. *"Everything* goes in his mouth. Drives me bat crazy."

"You know you're a pretty good dad."

"You're a pretty good mum." There was sincere love in his expression.

"You know…" Rhonda hesitated with a grin. "Sean probably won't wake up from his nap for another half hour or so… maybe we should *celebrate* our engagement."

"I think…" He looked at her slyly. "That we don't celebrate as often as we should these days."

"I think you're probably right."

"There is one more thing I need to do first." He paused as if to gather courage and got down on one knee in front of her. She held her breath in anticipation of the moment she'd secretly dreamed about since the first day she'd met him. "Rhonda Marie Kendrick, will you… marry me?"

"Yes, Kai Patrick Burton," she whispered, allowing the tears to fall from the corners of her eyes. "I *will* marry you."

With that, he reached up for her, and she reached down for him, and they pulled one another into an embrace that lasted at least a half an hour, maybe a little more.

CHAPTER TWELVE:
LIVE AT THE BRIDGESTONE ARENA

"What's all this?" Ian asked, throwing open the door to the men's room. Andy heaved again into the toilet and Nathanial moaned from the corner. "We're supposed to be on stage... in five minutes."

"I think he got sick because I did." Nathanial moaned again.

"It grossed me out." Andy leaned against the side of stall, brushing his shaggy hair off his forehead, which was covered in a sheen of sweat. "I was already terrified. Did you see how many people are out there?"

"You've performed before thousands more people than that."

"Not sober."

"You can handle it, mate. You've got to. We

have a sold-out house. You as well." Ian turned to Nathanial.

"I just don't know if I can, brotha'."

"You… you just *have* to." Ian told them. "It's our first show together. We're Buxton Peak."

Kai barged into the room. "What on bloody earth are you all doing?"

Ian was crouched near Andy, with one hand on his shoulder, and Nathanial was still sitting with his head between his knees.

"They're just nervous, that's all." Ian stood up and hoisted Andy off the floor. He dragged him over to the sink and turned on the faucet. "Splash some cold water on your face. Pull yourself together. We've got a show to do."

"Come here and help me get him off the floor," Kai asked. Ian walked over and together they each lifted one side of Nathanial. It wasn't easy to get that much man off the bathroom floor. They managed to get Nathanial up and one arm around each of their shoulders. That's how Jeremy found them when he pushed the door open.

"Well, you're a sorry bunch of musicians," Jeremy said. "You do realize you are due on stage, right?"

"We're working on it," Ian said. He and Kai tried to pull Nathanial forward, but it wasn't working well. He was just so much larger than they were.

"Ed," Jeremy called into his two-way radio. "Bring James and get over here. We need your assistance. We're in the men's room near the guys' dressing room. Nathanial's sick."

"Andy, too," Ian pointed out. Jeremy just frowned back at him and shook his head. The two long-time bodyguards must not have been far away, because within seconds James and Ed rushed in the door and hurried over to relieve Ian and Kai of the strain of holding Nathanial in a standing position. Andy was still leaning over the sink looking in the mirror at his slightly gray complexion.

Still propping Nathanial between him and James, Ed made a suggestion. "Mates, before every show, Ian and I take a few minutes and have a prayer together. I think it's about time the rest of you joined in on that."

"I'm an atheist."

"Shut up, Kai," Ian and Ed said in unison.

"Nathanial, you're a pastor." Ian walked over and looked right up into his new drummer's nervous face. "Would you be willing to pray for us?"

"I'm not sure I'm up for it, brotha'."

"Ian should do it," Andy whispered. "He's real good at prayin'. I've heard him." Everyone looked over at Andy. Although still weak, he was standing straight again. Ian walked over, put both hands on Andy's shoulders and looked him in the eye.

"I'd be honored, pal." He nodded at him in resolution. It felt reminiscent of the way he and Gary used to have a brief moment together before Ian would hand over the drumsticks. He whispered to his friend and bassist. "You can do this."

"Don't expect me to get down on my knees or something," Kai grumbled. Ian walked over to him and put his arm around Kai's shoulder. He wrapped his other arm around Jeremy's. He looked over at Andy and nodded, gesturing him to join them. They all came together in a circle of friends, heads slightly bowed, other than Kai, who just rolled his eyes. Ian took a slow breath, and a peace came over him.

"Heavenly Father," Ian started. Kai let out a frustrated sigh and Ian looked up at him with mild disgust. Kai looked away and furrowed his eyebrows like a teenager who was being forced to sit through a long sermon. Ian smiled slightly and bowed his head again. "We ask that Thou would be with us this evening and bring us comfort and strength. We know that we are just a bunch of hard, rock junkies..."

Andy gasped, and Ian looked up at him, startled out of his prayer. The hurt in his eyes was unmistakable, and Ian felt bad about his slip, using a word commonly used to describe drug users.

"Not that kind of junkies, mate." Ian apologized. "I just meant rock & roll addicts. Ugh, another bad choice of words. Uh… we're just a group of rock stars. Nothing more, nothing less."

Andy and Ian smiled slightly, nodded at one another, and bowed their heads again. Ian took another slow breath and started again.

"We know that what we will do tonight is nothing extraordinary and nothing important in the large scheme of life, but that it's important to us and to our fans. We ask that Thou would send Thy Spirit to be with us so that we can get through the fear and nervousness and perform the music that we've practiced. Please bless our families and friends and all who are with us tonight." Ian became choked up and couldn't continue for a moment. He cleared his throat and left a final thought. "And could you watch over Gary for us, too?"

Ian looked up briefly and caught Kai and Andy's attention. The three of them sort of smiled and nodded at one another. None of the others raised their eyes. It was as if they all knew that this was a private moment between the original band members, taking a few seconds to honor their lost friend. They bowed their heads again, and this time Kai even closed his eyes.

"We say these things in the name of Thy Son, our Savior, Jesus Christ," Ian whispered. "Amen." The rest of the guys in the circle echoed Ian's closing, all but Kai, who just smiled lightly. That was okay. It was as much as could be expected. They slowly pulled away from one another, dropping arms from around shoulders and stepping back.

Ian dragged Kai with him toward Nathanial and Andy. The four of them came together in a smaller circle and put their arms around each other again.

"This is it, guys," Ian whispered. "It's just the four of us on that stage. Ignore the people, ignore the lights, ignore the screaming teenage girls... and their mums who are pretending to be here only because their daughters need chaperones." The other guys chuckled.

"We've practiced these songs hundreds of times," Kai pointed out.

"And we're sober enough to remember them." Andy added with a grin.

"And we've got the blessings of heaven pourin' down upon us, thanks to our fearless leader prayin' for us." Nathanial leaned over and bumped his shoulder against Ian's.

"How can we possibly fail then?" Ian

bumped him right back and grinned up at him. "Let's rock."

"Let's rock," the guys echoed in unison. They each took a deep breath as they pulled away from one another and walked out of the restroom, with confidence in their steps and determination that they were going to blow away their sold-out audience.

*   *   *   *   *   *   *   *   *

It had been just over two years since Megan met Ian Taylor, yet this would be the second time she saw him perform live in concert. It wouldn't be the last. She decided to go with him for this first North American tour since they'd been married. There was no reason not to. There were no longer college classes to attend, and they didn't have children yet. After all her concern about not wanting to live in motor homes and hotel rooms, here she was packing to leave her beautiful new house and tour the continent.

Ian promised to take her to all the places they'd talked about: California, Temple Square, the St. Louis Arch, a Broadway show in New York City, and the Statue of Liberty. It would be a dream vacation with a few rock concerts thrown in for good measure. Vanessa decided to come along as well since she was in the beginning stages of pregnancy, and she would probably never get this opportunity after the baby came. Monique and Rhonda would stay in Nashville with their children, but they were here tonight because they were close to home at the Bridgestone Arena.

They brought little Taisha along for the afternoon festivities of watching the stage set-up and to watch daddy perform 'live' during rehearsals. They had even taken her on a tour of the whole arena and let her ride one of the Gators that took the workers all throughout the maze of tunnels under the stadium. She told her mom that it was one of the greatest adventures of her life. They had taken her up to the suite where the wives would watch most of the concert, and she bounced on the stadium seats of the private balcony and called out to hear the echo through the empty arena. Her best friend Jenny came along with her, and Jenny's mom took the girls and Rhonda's baby Sean home with her for an overnight play date. That gave Rhonda and Monique a much-needed break from motherhood to enjoy one night with their husbands before sending them off on their five-month concert tour.

Because they were officially 'on tour,' they booked luxury suites at the Omni Hotel in downtown Nashville and planned to party there after the show with Ed and India, who would also come on tour since she and Ed had married. Their manager, Jeremy, and a whole host of other entourage would be there as well. It was a slightly different group than in previous years, but they were more mature, more prepared, and on the right path for all of their lives.

"I've never seen anything like this." Monique leaned against the railing, looking down at the throngs of screaming fans awaiting the band's arrival. The pounding beats of the intro music and the beams of spotlights flashing through the air were perfectly timed so that they were part of the pre-show performance. "I never could have imagined when I met a hot, young seminary student who happened to like to play the drums, that someday I'd be standing in an arena full of screaming girls, waiting for him to come out onstage and perform for them."

"I know exactly what you mean." Megan smiled over at her new friend and winked. "I had no idea what I was getting myself into when I fell in love with Ian."

"I wonder what's taking them so long." Rhonda came up behind them and looked over the railing at the empty stage. "They're running really late."

"They're probably picking Nathanial off the floor in the bathroom." Monique laughed and the other ladies turned to her in shock. "He gets really nervous before performing."

"You're kidding." Vanessa's southern accent punctured the conversation. "He's always seemed so confident to me."

"You should have seen him the night we first met y'all." Monique turned to Megan and Rhonda. "He tossed up that whole New York Strip he had eaten at the steakhouse. He was so excited."

"He threw up because he was excited?" Megan asked. "That doesn't make sense."

"Well, excited and nervous. Can you imagine if one of the most famous rock bands in the world walked up to you and said 'come join our band'? You'd be nervous, too."

"Yeah, I guess you're right." Megan turned her attention back into the arena.

"You were pretty darn nervous that night in Copenhagen when Ian dragged you out onto the stage and sang to you." Rhonda taunted Megan slightly, grinning over at her.

"I thought I was going to pass out," Megan said.

"See, so you do understand," Monique said.

With a grin on her face, India rushed through the door of their private suite. Her breathlessness and playful expression implied that she'd rushed up here with gossip. "They're almost ready," she said. "A couple of the guys got sick."

"Who?" Megan asked, knowing immediately it wasn't Ian. He didn't get nervous before his shows. He was in a zone, radiating confidence from his whole being.

"Nathanial," Monique guessed correctly.

"I wouldn't be surprised if Andy was sick as well." Vanessa added.

"You are both correct." India laughed.

"I doubt Kai was." Rhonda shook her head, a secret smile playing into her eyes. "He left the house in a *very* good mood this morning."

"I'll bet he did." Megan teased her best friend and pushed her shoulder lightly. "How many *hours* ago did you guys get married?"

"Twenty-two hours ago, actually." Rhonda ceremoniously looked down at her watch with a grin.

"Congratulations, by-the-way." Monique reached over and gave her a hug.

"Hey, I haven't seen that ring yet!" India rushed forward and pulled Rhonda's hand over so she could get a good look at the enormous diamond resting there. "It's so beautiful."

"Thanks." Rhonda smiled, looking down at her hand with a sigh. "I still can't believe this is real. I don't even want to know how much it cost."

"About as much as that mansion he bought

you." Monique shook her head in mock disgust, teasing with a smile.

"Pretty soon you're going to be able to afford a house like that." Megan suggested.

"I like the house I live in right now, thank-you-very-much," Monique said. "I like my neighborhood and the school my daughter attends, and I like my church."

"How about this." Megan cleared her throat, rephrasing her approach. "You're going to have a lot more money to support the causes you believe in, *for instance* your church."

"Now *that* I could handle." The two women smiled at one another. For the past few months they worked side by side, spending Ian's money and improving the youth center. After this, Monique would have her own money to work with. Megan understood; that would feel good.

The lights lowered and the music faded. The crowd knew exactly what was about to happen, and they screamed for the band they loved, the anticipation almost palpable. As was tradition for every show, Kai's guitar solo pierced through the crowd for several seconds before Andy's bass boomed in, adding beat and soul. With no hesitation, Nathanial struck the drum set with an intensity that Buxton Peak fans had never experienced. They cheered with enthusiasm for him alone, welcoming him to their fandom.

"Hello, Nashville!" Ian cried into the microphone, and the crowd screamed again. With no more introduction than that, he began the first song in their set. It was a powerful, hard tune that the fans knew well and sang along with. It was the same, yet different. There was an edge to the beat that came along with a new drummer and a new dynamic.

The crowd seemed to love the alteration and cheered in appreciation that *their* band was once again performing live. To the ears of the adoring crowd, this music was created for them and them alone. The music that was imagined by Ian, improved by Kai and Andy, and perfected by Nathanial. *This* was Buxton Peak.

ABOUT THE AUTHOR

Julie L. Spencer lives in the central Michigan area with her husband and teenage children. She has a very full life managing a conservation district office, writing grant proposals, newsletters, articles, and book reviews. Julie has been writing since she was in junior high, but prior to publishing her first novel, *The Cove*, her only published work was her master's thesis. She loves to read and write New Adult Contemporary Clean fiction and has several more novels and non-fiction projects in the works.

Like *Buxton Peak Book Three: The End of the Beginning?*

Please leave a review on Julie's Author Page on Amazon and Goodreads!

Other books by Julie L. Spencer:

Buxton Peak Book One: Who Is Ian Taylor?

Buxton Peak Book Two: Center Stage

The Cove

Julie loves to hear from her readers and can be reached at juliespencer1998@gmail.com

Follow Julie on Twitter @juliespencer98
www.facebook.com/JulieLSpencerAuthorPage

Check out Julie's blog at:
http://opinions-are-just-that.blogspot.com/

Bonus:
Sneak Peak of

The Cove
Julie L. Spencer

CHAPTER ONE: TODD

"Why did you do that?" Gail stood in his lit doorway, dripping wet in her designer swimsuit. Todd kept the screen door closed between them, anger in his eyes and a scowl on his face. Gail pushed the door open and stomped into his house, leaving water all across his linoleum floor. He closed his eyes, took a deep breath, then grabbed the kitchen towel from the handle on the stove. As he stooped down to wipe up the mess, she grabbed her long hair in her hands and wrung the water from it so that it left an even bigger pool of water beside her. He paused, clenched his hand around the towel and wiped up that mess as well. When Todd stood up, he tossed the towel at Gail's chest.

"Dry yourself off." Todd snapped at her. "You're making a mess in my kitchen." He walked back over to the counter where he had been making himself a sandwich. *How can he possibly be hungry after all that food at the country club?*

"Why did you have to show up there anyway?" Gail demanded.

"I was invited!" Todd turned back to her with fierceness in his eyes. "By your *fiancé!*" He spat the words at her and she flinched back from his accusing eyes. He stepped away from the counter and crossed the room to her. She was glad he'd put down the knife he'd used to cut the salami for his sandwich. Not that she thought he would ever really get so mad he might hurt her, it just would have felt a little more threatening.

"Stephan invited...you? Why?" He ignored her question.

"Do you have *any* idea how much Patrick loves you? How much it's going to hurt him when he finds out that you're *engaged* to someone else?"

She backed away from him, turned and walked into the dining room, looking around for someplace she could sit that wouldn't leave a wet stain. Todd followed her and seemed to anticipate what she needed. He moved a stack of books off a dining room chair that was vinyl or plastic or some other surface she didn't really care to know about. Nothing in her sheltered little world would contain anything so *cheap*, but at that moment she didn't really care. She was just glad to get off her feet.

Gail suddenly realized how tired she was, not just from swimming but from the whole day. Without really consciously thinking about it, she realized she was tired from the past few weeks, months, maybe years. She was just tired. She rested her arms on the table and leaned her head forward. He left the room and came back with a big, fluffy towel and draped it around her shoulders.

"Thanks." She looked up at him. The scornful expression still had not left his face. That hard look in his eyes told her he was far more angry with her than she was with him.

Patrick was Todd's best friend, had been since a Boy Scout trip in their early teens. They had hung out at every Stake activity, every Youth Conference, every camping trip. They were best buddies, and Gail had just hurt his best buddy more than she'd ever hurt anyone before. The tricky part was…Patrick didn't even *know* about it yet. He was still serving as a missionary in the Philippines.

It was the classic case of girl waiting for her missionary, girl meeting another guy who already returned from his mission, girl being wooed into a relationship quicker than she knew what hit her, and girl being proposed to at a dance.

"I didn't mean to say yes…"

"*What?*"

Gail flinched away from Todd's demanding glare.

"Well, what would you do if someone proposed to you in front of two hundred people?" she asked in exasperation. "Including your mom and dad!" She buried her face in her arms again and started crying. He stood there for a moment, then she heard him stomp from the room. When he came back he set something on the table beside her.

"Here!" He snapped when she didn't look up. She raised her head and gratefully accepted a box of tissues. "How did you get here, anyway?"

"I swam." Gail sniffed and wiped her nose.

"All the way across the cove?"

"It's not that far." She grabbed a couple more tissues and dried the remaining tears. "I train everyday and swim at least that and more."

"Yeah, but that's in a pool. Isn't it a little different?"

"Not really." She sat up a little straighter and began towel-drying her hair. She wanted to be angry still, but decided she really didn't have that much to be angry about. She was more embarrassed than anything else. There she had been, dancing with Stephan at the country club when suddenly he had hopped up on the band stand, grabbed the microphone from the lead singer, stopped the band and called out to her across the room.

Gail was petrified when she realized what he was about to do. She was rooted to her spot on the dance floor but looked over at where her mom and dad were sitting. They were beaming! They loved Stephan. He was everything they would ever want for their little girl. He was in his last year of college, worked at her father's firm, had been home from his mission for three years, and was ready to settle down. He came from a good family, which translated in her parents' minds as a *rich* family, was handsome and confident and someone they could trust to take care of their daughter.

Gail had reached her hand up to her neck as if to grasp the set of pearls that rested there. And Stephan had asked her to marry him. She felt tears fall from her eyes as a completely different future flashed in front of her. A future filled with parties just like this one, filled with an extravagant home and children who were just as beautiful as Stephan. *A future without Patrick.* She was so uncertain at that moment, with everyone staring at her waiting for her reply.

She had smiled back at Stephan and nodded her head, agreeing to marry him. He ran across the room and swooped her up in his arms. He swung her around and the audience cheered. Gail couldn't help smiling and laughing until he put her down and she caught the eye of someone she never would have expected to see at the country club. There, on the other side of the room, standing with a plate of appetizers in one hand and a glass of punch in the other, was Todd.

Gail hadn't seen Todd since Patrick left for his mission. Todd was best friends with Patrick. Her missionary. The boy she had planned to wait for. The boy she had known and loved since their days in Primary. The boy who was counting on her to be there when he got home, just four short months from now. Was four months so long to wait? Could she not endure that long? She realized it wasn't even that she couldn't wait. She never had intended for any of this to happen.

Gail had met Stephan in the gym at the college where they were both students. He knew that she swam every morning, and he knew that he wanted to meet her. Conveniently, he decided that he needed to swim every morning at that same time.

Gradually, they became friends and realized their parents were both members of the same country club, and Stephan worked in her father's law firm.

Gail started spending time with Stephan and they went to dances together and to parties at the club. Every church activity she attended, he was there. Every Institute class, every sacrament meeting. Suddenly he was everywhere she was, and she didn't seem to mind. Stephan was a great guy. He encouraged her with her swimming, and her studies, and was just an all-around decent man. But...he wasn't Patrick.

Gail had continued to write to Patrick faithfully all along. She had always been careful not to get too romantic in her letters. She'd been warned not to do that to missionaries. They needed to concentrate on their work. She really hadn't even made any firm commitments to Patrick before he left. There was just an unspoken connection. They had held hands at recess in elementary school. They had gone to prom together. They had been each others' first kiss. They had loved one another longer than either of them could remember. They were comfortable together.

Up until that night, Gail's letters to Patrick had gone out once a week for the past year and a half. What was going to happen now? Would she write him a "Dear John" letter like she'd heard so many other girls had done? She needed some good advice. She felt confusion mix with her exhaustion and she laid her head back on her arms and closed her eyes.

"How do you know Stephan, anyway?" Gail suddenly looked up at Todd. It occurred to her she knew very little about what Todd had been doing since the last time she'd talked to him over a year and a half ago at Patrick's farewell.

"I have a couple of classes with Stephan at the college." He sat down across from her.

"Are you in business school then?" she asked. She doubted it. He didn't look like the corporate type. He was tall and solid. He was tanned like he spent a lot of time outdoors.

"Economics, with a minor in Business Administration. I'm in my senior year, but probably won't graduate till December. I'm a little behind still."

"Seriously?" she asked. "You're awfully young, aren't you? How did you get through college so fast?"

"I'm older than you think I am." Todd leaned his arm against the table. "I'm three years older than Patrick. I just served in Venture Scouts well into my college years because I lived at home while I was going to school. So, I stayed really close to the guys. Plus I got two years in at the college before I went on my mission."

"Hmmm, you'd think I would have known that. I've known you for years."

"You're kind of caught up in your own little world."

"What are you saying? That I'm a snob and don't pay attention to the people around me?" She stuck her chin in the air, slightly offended yet realizing there may be a ring of truth to it.

"No, I'm just saying you're really busy with all of your…activities."

"You don't approve of how much time I spend at the pool, do you?"

"I think it's honorable that you want to achieve so much. The Olympics were a big deal. You impressed the heck out of all of us." He paused. "You know I attended almost every meet you had locally, with Patrick?"

"I didn't know that, sorry."

"Like I said, you're busy."

"Do you work? Or are you finishing school first?" she asked.

"I'm a builder. I'd like to own my own company someday. That's why I'm going to business school."

That would explain the tan and the physique. It occurred to Gail she was sort of staring at him with a little wonder on her face. She felt her cheeks heat up and looked away.

"What are you going to do now?" Todd asked.

"I don't know." Gail let out a tired sigh, then stood up to leave. "I'll have to think about that. Don't say anything to Patrick about this yet, okay? Or Stephan."

"All right," he said, pushing back from the table. "I should probably drive you home though. You look like you're about ready to fall over from exhaustion." He led her out of his tiny cottage and helped her climb up into his Ford F-250.

It seemed a little strange to Gail that Todd had such meager accommodations, yet a brand new, fancy truck with all the features and gadgets a guy could ever want.

As he walked around the car, she couldn't help draw in a deep breath and lean her head back against the leather seat. His truck smelled amazing. The mixture of new-car smell and whatever cologne he wore was intoxicating. When Todd got into the truck, he didn't seem to notice she was impressed with it. It seemed like it was just a truck to him. *Maybe he needs a big truck for his work as a builder. It's probably a guy thing.*

It took longer than she would have thought to follow the coastline back to her house, and it occurred to her that the cove probably was larger than she realized. Still, the swim had felt good. It hadn't been too far. She was an experienced swimmer, an Olympic gold medalist with a world record in the 400 meter freestyle.

She had been approached by several sponsors after her most recent win, but had settled on Speedo and All Sport. She had always worn Speedo's swimwear and knew the quality and styles. She felt comfortable endorsing them, and they had offered her a lot of money to pose for photo shoots. Also, she liked one of All Sport's sports drinks and she just wanted to support what she used.

Gail had renounced her collegiate eligibility in order to cash in on endorsement offers, but felt it was cool that so many sponsors had approached her. She drifted off in her own thoughts as they drove, and she realized she kind of thought of herself as a little invincible when it came to swimming. Pulling into her driveway brought her out of her daze.

"Don't take me all the way to the house," she asked him.

"Why? Are you embarrassed to be seen with me?"

"No." She laughed. "I just left my clothes down by the water. I took off that stifling dress before launching myself into the lake to come over and yell at you." Something about telling him that made her blush again, and she wondered why she should feel bashful around him. He was just a friend. A friend of her boyfriend...well former boyfriend. And a friend of her...fiancé. That was going to take some getting used to.

"Um, just curious..." He pulled around the bend of her driveway, completing a perfect three-point turn rather than start up the hill towards the house. "Were you wearing your swimsuit under your dress? I probably shouldn't have asked you that. I'm sorry. I'm just dead curious." He stammered on until Gail was doubled over with laughter.

"Of course I had my swimsuit on. I always have a swimsuit on. I pretty much live in one. You don't have to be embarrassed." She jumped down out of his truck and ran lightly across the grass to where her heap of clothes lay by the seawall. She picked up her heels and dress from the dew covered grass and turned back to wave goodbye to Todd. He was already backing up to finish his turn back down the driveway and out of her world.

Gail's attention was drawn back to the dark water of the cove, then up the hill to her home and the country club next door. Gail had grown up at that club, had learned to swim, had first been approached by a coach who wanted to train with her. The party there was still in full swing. Party was a relative term anyway. What her parents and their friends did was mainly dancing and eating. That had been the plan for her evening as well.

It was interesting how her life had taken a drastic turn. What had started as a casual relationship with a nice man had suddenly become an engagement. Her planned future with Patrick had vanished into a distant dream. A new future loomed in front of her and she had gone from being Patrick's girlfriend to being Stephan's fiancé.

She smiled and sighed in contentment as she thought of Stephan. He was an amazing man and someone she would be proud to call her own. She thought of the smile on his face as she agreed to become his wife, but her thoughts quickly turned to Todd's face as he realized what had happened. The anger she remembered changed in her mind to a calm expression of understanding. She wondered why her thoughts would take such a sudden turn. Gail's eyes were once again drawn to the cove and across the lake to the small cottage where Todd's truck was just pulling into his driveway.

Check out Amazon.com to read more of
The Cove by Julie L. Spencer